AF291130

Gino Leineweber

Immersion in the Dhamma

*My Experiences with an
American Buddhist Monk*

Verlag Expeditionen

Gino Leineweber
Immersion in the Dhamma
My Experiences with an
American Buddhist Monk

First Edition 2018
Cover Photo: Attila Joo; Berlin, Germany
Cover Design:
Birgitta Sjöblom, Salzwedel; Germany
Copy Editor:
Barry Stevenson, Hamburg; Germany

ISBN 978-3-943863-88-8

There is no wisdom
Without meditation
There is no meditation
Without wisdom

Table of Contents

Prolog

It happened in 1999 that I met Bhante Yoga-vacara Rahula after being told to visit him by Frank Wesendahl, who was running a Buddhist meditation center in Roseburg about 40 kilometers east of Hamburg, Germany.

I was asking Frank about a meditation course I wanted to attend and knew nothing about Rahula, except that he was an American Buddhist monk.

Rahula had written a book about how he had become a monk, which I later read. One might ask why I wanted to write a book about him and I can only reply that how he became a monk is interesting but I know him mainly as a teacher whose Western background might well be the fundamental factor in the significant influence on his students that his teaching exerts. Although equipped with outstanding intellectual skills, he has not focused on publishing writings about Buddhism, as others thankfully do, but on offering guidance in its practice.

In the meantime, I have come to know him well and appreciate him as a person who conducts his life on twin journeys: the one through this life on earth and the other on the Noble Eightfold Path, the Buddhist way to liberation, namely the way to overcome *Samsara*, the "cyclicality of all life, matter, and existence" that will lead to attaining enlightenment.

However, he does not walk this path alone. He offers his students support, guidance and company on their own journey along it.

After the first retreat with Bhante Rahula, I have almost never missed meeting him whenever he visits Germany and it has become a welcome routine for me to drive him to various places. I have also visited him in the United States and, largely because of this book, in Sri Lanka, where he was ordained as a monk in 1977. There is a third journey I wish to narrate in this book, namely the travels that I have undertaken in his company.

In order to complete this book, I talked to other Buddhist monks, interviewed some of Rahula's friends and family members, as well as asking some of his students about him for further information.

I am very grateful for the support that I received. I would particularly like to thank the highly esteemed Bhante Gunnaratana, the abbot of a forest monastery in West Virginia, where Bhante Rahula used to live as vice-abbot for 23 years, and Bhante Ariyajothi, the abbot of the monastery in Unawatuna, who supported Rahula when he wanted to stay in solitude for a while in that little village. I would also like to express my gratitude to Mali Gaudi, Klaus and Miyako Habich, Gabrielle Heinemann, Angelika Post und Frank Wesendahl as representative of all the other contributors in Germany, the United States and Sri Lanka.

Finally I want to express special thanks to Rahula's mother, Virginia DuPrez, who not only talked to me about her son, but also gave me accommodation when I visited her in Riverside, California.

On being asked sometimes why I was going to write a book about Bhante Rahula when he had already written a wonderful autobiography about his becoming a monk, I replied that this book would be neither a biography nor a book about Buddhism: it would be (and is, after all said and done) a travel book.

I hope the reader will appreciate the journeys as much as I did.

Gino Leineweber
June 2018

> *Today I am reborn*
> *The first day of the rest of my life*
> Bhante Rahula,
> after a meditation course
> in Nepal, 1973

Chapter 1

Four comes after three and then, of course, five comes after four. However, is that really true? Does not two follow three? What is the meaning of the numbers, anyway? When the three tumbles over, is it still a number or the letter m? Am I here or am I there? Am I, anyhow? What is reality? What is imagination? When was the beginning? When will the end be? Lacking the answers for directions, meanings, space and time, we have to remove things from our conditioned perceptions.

We set a beginning and an end to all movement, which is only a concept without exact clues as to what they are. The only conclusion we can draw is that, if there is a beginning, an end is inevitable. Starting to walk implies a halt.

'I wish you luck on your path'; the Venerable Bhante Rahula, an American Buddhist monk wrote that acknowledgement on the first page of my copy of his autobiography *One Night Shelter*. What path? I did not then realize I had already started on one. But I had. What he meant, of course, was the Noble Eightfold Path and I was already on it. For the first time I was aware; I just had not realized the beginning.

Eight steps. What is the first? What will be the last? Are there even any at all? In Buddhist teaching, all the steps are equally necessary. The Path essentially is the last part of the Four Noble Truths and if you intend to take the Noble Eightfold Path, you need to comprehend the Four Noble Truths that signify the aim of the historic Buddha's teaching, namely to overcome suffering.

The fact of *Dukkha* (suffering) is the first of the Four Noble Truths: that human beings grasp and cling to the body, the mind and the external world. Under the influence of ignorance, attachments and cravings arise that lead inevitably, sooner or later, to sorrow, confusion, pain, grief and despair. To understand that life can be suffering, which refers to *Anicca* (impermanence) and *Anatta* (non-self), namely the impermanent, the unstable and the non-self of conditioned existence, is the very foundation of *Dhamma*, the Buddha's teachings.

The second truth is to know the causes of suffering, henceforth in short: greed, ignorance and hatred. If there are causes, then you can find a way to finally overcome them, which means the third and final way to do so: the Noble Eightfold Path.

"The crucial turning point in my life was when, fortunately, my mind was ready to understand, with the aid of some serious reflections, the full meaning and implications of the Four Noble Truths. It was what you might call a spiritual rebirth."

That was Bhante Rahula's reply when I asked him about the beginning of his path. A monk in the *Theravada* tradition of Buddhism is usually called *Bhante*, in other traditions, as in the Tibetan for example, *Lama* or *Rinpoche*. As a form of respect, using the word 'venerable' is considered appropriate. The Venerable Bhante Yogavacara Rahula was, of course, not always a monk and not always venerable either. His former name appears on his birth certificate: Scott Joseph DuPrez, and he was born on June 21st, 1948.

I met him first in 1999 in the House of Silence (Haus der Stille), a Buddhist Meditation Center in Germany. I might have just read his name in the program I was leafing through in front of the warden Frank Wesendahl. He had experienced Rahula's courses, visited him in the forest monastery *Bhavana Society* in West Virginia, in the United States, and traveled with him, including a hiking tour in the Grand Canyon. He, for sure, knew Rahula.

I had liked Frank from the beginning when I had called to check the venue and program, long before a retreat I went on with another teacher I had first. That conversation on the telephone was, as it turned out, the only opportunity we had to speak at any length. The retreat, however, was a common meditation course in Noble Silence. The participants are not supposed to communicate either during the sessions or at any other time. In the meantime, I have shared in a good number of such retreats and a lot of them with almost the same participants. Even, after years of spending so much time together, I, for one, still do not really know their names properly. The purpose of this silence is to provide support for the inner process of practice.

It was at that moment, while Frank and I were talking about my future participation in the retreats, that he looked at me, took a guess and said: ”Go to Rahula”. He recommended him because of his own experience and thought it would be suitable for me as well. And he was right.

I had been participating for about three years in a so-called psychodynamic, body-oriented and spiritual therapeutic group. It helped me in a way to understand myself from a psychological aspect. What I liked most about the classes were the different kinds of meditation methods that were on offer to practice with. That led me to my own studies on meditation and I found a very good book on the subject, very thorough: the famous *Orange Book* by Osho, and in it I found *Vipassana*. If I were to name a starting point on my path, that would be it.

Vipassana meditation is a practice which consciously uses breathing, thoughts, feelings, and actions to gain insight into the true nature of reality: impermanence, suffering, and the realization of the non-self (*Anicca, Dukkha, Anatta*). I did not know that well at that time, but liked the feeling of mindfulness. I was not aware either the very first time I practiced *Vipassana* that it would open the gateway to Buddhist teaching. Not only for me was *Vipassana* the beginning, however. It was also the start for Bhante Rahula, way back when he was traveling in Asia in the 1970s and came into contact with the spirituality of the old Asian culture. It was the time of the hippies, when hundreds and hundreds of young women and men traveled around the world especially in search of 'peace and happiness', a quest which was, however, mostly drug-related.

Against this background, a group of four friends left the state of California, where they had grown up. One of them was Scott DuPrez, who just had graduated, gaining his first degree in college. In direct contrast to what his parents wanted, namely for him to finish his next two years at university, he had this to say: "I wanted to go on this around-the-world adventure to see how other people lived and perhaps discover something inside me or about myself which would open up new horizons or a direction to take".

We can take it for granted that not only on a journey will you know in advance what is going to happen to you. Just in retrospect you can tell. Then, however, considering what did happen, you realize, that everything could only have occurred the way it did. Otherwise you would not be the same person. It means in a way, that life is predetermined. Whatever happens follows a certain move that depends on different abilities, like the potentials someone has or the environment. For young Scott was to become a Buddhist monk; nobody could tell that in advance, but there was a potential, there were signs that he might change his life dramatically.

Born and raised in Riverside, a town south of Los Angeles, he had a commonplace childhood and youth in an everyday American family, with a tractor salesman for a father, a schoolteacher for a mother, and two older siblings: a brother and a sister. The family attended the local Methodist Church and the children the Sunday school.

Scott used to be a Boy Scout, joined the Y.M.C.A., and went on camping and surfing trips. On his sixteenth birthday, his parents bought him a car; he drove to the beach in or went cruising the streets in with his friends. He went to parties, started drinking beer and wine, had various girl friends and enjoyed his adolescence. It was the era of cultural revolution and the hippie movement. It implied experimentation and promoted the popularity of marijuana and LSD. He was conditioned by that eventful period with its pop and rock music, long hair, faded Levis and T-shirts and its more casual free lifestyle for youth.

During that joyful time he first heard the name 'Buddha'. On one of his surfing excursions down in Baja California in Mexico, he was walking these little streets full of shops for tourists. As he was passing one of the many handicraft stores, he noticed a clay statue, about 30 centimeters high. He bought it and put it on top of his television, using it as a rack for his hats. He had not known the meaning of the figurine until his mother looked at it and said,

"Oh, what's this? You bought that in Mexico? It's a statue of Buddha."

"Who's Buddha?"

"Go, look in the encyclopedia," she said.

He did; he looked it up, and read a little bit about the Buddha. However, it did not do anything for him at that time. When he was walking down the streets with all these shops in Mexico selling pottery, his attention was suddenly caught by this very statue that was sitting above all these others, these matadors, bulls, cats and so on. He almost felt, he told me, that the statue was doing this on purpose and making a gesture with its finger: come!

"I walked over," he said, "and thought it was interesting and I wanted to buy it. And I talked to the guy and I did. And then I saw it every day whenever I walked into my room. It might have had some kind of effect on me."

What effect, you cannot tell. I do not want to put too much into it. However, in a way, it was the first step to his ordination later as a Buddhist monk. The Buddha, from that moment on, meant something to him, may even have mattered in an unconscious way. I myself had a similar experience when I went with a friend on a round trip in northern Thailand in the 1980s. A female guide took us to different temples every day and we, behind her back, made fun of the way she pronounced the word 'temple'. I still have that sound in my ears. At that time, I had no idea about Buddha either. Nevertheless, the temples were nice, colorful, well designed and I loved visiting them. There was indeed something that stuck in my mind out of all the information. Some temples have paintings depicting episodes in the life of the historic Buddha, from his birth as Siddhartha Gautama, through his enlightenment to his death. The saying goes, after his birth as a son of a king, it was predicted that he would become either a great king or a great holy man. His father wanted the former for him and decided to protect him from religious teachings and the knowledge of human suffering. When Gautama turned sixteen, his father had him married to a cousin of the same age and Gautama later had a son by her. The name of the son, by the way, was Rahula.

Although Siddhartha was provided with everything he could want or need, he left the palace at the age of twenty-nine and realized what his father had been trying to hide from him, namely sickness, aging and suffering. These depressed him, and he quit his life as a prince to pursue one rather as an ascetic, begging for alms in the streets, in order to overcome aging, sickness, and death. He practiced under the guidance of two teachers and achieved high levels of meditative awareness. Nevertheless, he was not satisfied. He moved on, took his austerities further and entered a period of extreme ascetic practice by depriving himself of food and sleep. After almost starving himself to death, he collapsed in a river while bathing. Had it not been for his rescue by a village girl, he would have drowned. She afterwards provided him with some food, which restored Siddhartha's energy. He then reconsidered his path and, sensing its futility, began meditating with the profound determination to understand the truth of human existence. It was then that he realized the need to avoid these two extremes: sensual indulgence, passions and luxury on the one hand and severe asceticism, austerity and mortification on the other. Doing so would lead to the Middle Path, which produces insight and knowledge and tends towards calmness and serenity. He then sat himself under the Bodhi tree, and vowed never to arise until he had found the truth. Forty-nine days of meditation later, while at the age of thirty-five, he attained Enlightenment, which means having gained complete insight into the cause of suffering and the steps necessary to eliminate it. These discoveries became known as the Four Noble Truths. To master these truths, it is believed that *Nirvana*, a state of supreme liberation, is possible for any human being. The Buddha, after his awakening, began teaching the way to overcome suffering, the Noble Eightfold Path.

What I kept in mind concerning the Buddha, as I learned the meaning of the pictures on the walls of the temples, was that he had left his palace and changed his life after seeing all the suffering. But this was in no way a significant impact that changed my future life any more than the clay Buddha was for Rahula either. It could have been a knock at the door that one day might be answered.

Is enlightenment something you can attain? Or is it something that already exists? Or more correctly: Is enlightenment an aim?

Bhante Rahula asked me one day: "Do you know why I gave my autobiography the title *One Night Shelter?*"

I did not know, so he supplied the answer:

"I gave it as a description about impermanence. It is about everything we do in life. From the time we are born to the time we die is just a sequence of changing conditions. You are a baby for a while, then a child and later a teenager and then you are a young adult, you know. You meet your boy scouts, your students, and all the various things you do. But all that changes and all our identity is changing in that too. Even the desires and the hopes that we have and other experiences, maybe having a girlfriend or a boyfriend or other things, it is just a "one night shelter". It is a temporary place for your mind to get attached to and then it changes. And then you have to go on. No experience lasts more than a night—that's to say 'night' as a metaphor. And that's what I've tried to describe in the book, because of all the things I was doing: drugs, being a hippie, a Boy Scout, joining the army, you know, traveling, all that was just in the mind and added to my experience. And then, when I heard the *Dhamma*, I was able to reflect on all these things and it made much more sense."

When I read the book, I did not know that. Anyway, it does not matter since I understood the meaning while reading; incidentally, that kind of thing matters, for the writer as well as for the reader.

Anyway, I did not get my first impressions of his background from his autobiography but rather from his narration during the retreat in the House of Silence. This house is located in the little village east of Hamburg. The two main buildings, the main house dating from 1903 and the meditation hall build in 1970, lie between ponds and old trees, offer sufficient space for not only practicing walking meditation but also for peaceful rest between classes. And, of course, also space for a lot of work as I learned when attending the first meditation seminar and volunteering for gardening at the required daily working hour.

When I went on my first retreat with Rahula, I was already acquainted with the venue. After arriving, I went to the meditation hall to choose and prepare my place of meditation for the next ten days. On that occasion, I first met Bhante Rahula in person. He was preparing the room, especially the arrangement of the mats for the twenty plus participants. What I saw was a skinny monk wearing the obligatory orange robe, very convincing in his wishes about the interior, and yet possessing a calm and friendly voice that matched his whole appearance.

The seminar not having officially started at this point, I wondered if I would be lucky enough to exchange a few words with him, but apart from 'hello', that was it. It appeared a bit strange to me because at that time I was still in the habit of engaging in small talk whenever I met anyone and not familiar with the concept of Right Speech. As a result, I was a little disappointed. However, during that very seminar, I learned why 'hello' sufficed—it was because nothing else was needed.

I chose a seat by the wall a little beside the direct view to the monk's place. Here I spent the next ten days in meditation and listened to the lectures, listened to a monk who taught mindfulness, and not only taught it, but, as I have since become aware, lived it as well. When I first laid eyes on Bhante Rahula, his calmness impressed me and it was only later that I became aware of its significance, namely that the way he talks and acts is based on mindfulness.

In his teachings, he took examples from his own experience and explained the natural world in the light of the *Dhamma*. From that, I learned he had grown up in Riverside, California. California! What a wonderful impression that place had already made on my mind thanks to all those books and movies. And he grew up there! I immediately saw him in my mind's eye, a carefree individual in a liberal educational system, enjoying childhood and adolescence with friends and family, spending his free time outdoors, making jokes and going surfing. The surfing part in my imagination was more a daily routine than it was in reality, which was more like one trip every two weeks. I had not realized before that his hometown was some 50 miles distant from the Pacific Ocean. Anyway it is a pleasant, run-of-the-mill American town. Visitors coming from the direction of the major conurbation Los Angeles, which is located in the northwest, are welcomed to Riverside, a city of over 300,000 residents, by the 1,331-foot high Mount Rubidoux. The area by the side of the Santa Ana River consists of parkland with over three miles of trails with an extensive view all over the city. Rahula's family moved a couple of times, mostly due to his mother's school teaching job, within and around Riverside. At the time he was born, the family lived in Brawley, a small town situated about 20 or 30 miles from the Mexican border and just south of Salton Sea, the largest lake in California.

"It's a saltwater lake," Bhante Rahula once told me, when we were at a scenic point in Joshua Tree National Park and he pointed at a lake far away, "it's very low. The lake's below sea level; Brawley is in the area were we used to live. There was a lot of farming around there. Imperial County, where it is located, was a rich farming area. They got the water from the Colorado River and harvested a lot of vegetables. That's where my father was working, selling farm machinery and then, later, cars. Salesman, all his life. My mother as a schoolteacher made more money than my father did."

He is partly of French descent on his father's side. His grandfather and great-grandfather came from France, hence the name DuPrez, one of the ancient Huguenot names. His paternal grandmother came from Colorado, where his father was born, from a family with a farming background, but his father left for California when he was young.

Some American history comes shining through on his mother's side: her family originally came from England and, going back eight generations, was part of the Puritan exodus; they left England and later became Quakers. The eighth great-grandfather came with the Quakers to Pennsylvania when William Penn, an English real estate entrepreneur and philosopher, established the first Quaker colonies.

When I talked to Rahula about his descent, I concluded that he was on one side a farmer by blood and on the other 'of noble stock'.

"Yeah, basically," he agreed, "English and French bloodline. My mother was born in Los Angeles and, I guess, when my father came out to California, he met my mother there after the war. My mother's family lived in Los Angeles. That's where my mother was born.

And then they lived in San Diego for some time."

The significant move the family made, happened to be to a cul-de-sac almost in the middle of the city of Riverside when Rahula was in seventh grade. The house is a one-story building with a double garage door on the left and a big tree in front of the house on the sidewalk on the right. It has a red roof with mostly beige-colored walls and on the boardwalk a nice painting with the American flag, an island with two palm trees on it and the house number: 5368. From here he biked to the nearby Sierra Junior High School. In this environment he spent a lot of time with his friends and schoolmates. His friendship with some of them, the ones he later traveled or joined the army with, has lasted down the years.

Rahula, luckily as far as I can see, was fortunate to be blessed with loving parents that seemed to be understanding, caring, demanding no more than they needed to and providing him with a happy childhood. He was a typical Californian child with good grades, doing sports in school and starting to surf at the age of 13. He had long hair, wore faded Levis and T-shirts, as typical an all-American boy from an all-American family with roots to European immigrants as anyone could wish.

He started consuming drugs one day during his adolescence. He also did it at home in his bedroom with friends while listening to his stereo. This could not really be concealed from his parents, because they could smell it. His mother, at that time, was a vice-principal at one of the more rowdy junior high schools in Riverside and was very aware of the drug situation in general. She was confronted with pot smokers that came to school stoned and even sold drugs to the other kids and also with kids crazed out of their skulls on LSD or angel dust. She was alert to all the signs and could guess fairly well by the way he acted sometimes that he was also a user.

He first experienced drugs while on a surfing expedition down in Mexico with a group of friends. By and by, he was smoking pot quite regularly along with taking 'reds' and 'speed' from time to time and drinking beer.

When he graduated from high school in 1966, America was deeply involved in the war in Vietnam and the carefree time Rahula spent in Riverside as a young man was interrupted by his having to serve in the army. Many of his friends were already getting drafted and he guessed he would be next.

In December 1967, therefore, while in junior college studying the new field of data processing and computer science, he committed himself, joined by a friend named Dave, to serve for three years instead of the usual two for draftees because volunteering would give him the opportunity to choose the type of training he wanted. Unlike most draftees, who were sent into the infantry, he chose training in electronics. After boot camp and advanced training, he was sent to the NATO forces in Germany, where, during the summer of 1969, he received notice of his coming transfer to South Vietnam.

Before he complied with the order to fly to Vietnam, he took two weeks' leave and visited some friends who had been drafted around the same time that he had joined up and were now already discharged from active military service.

Dave was also back. He had been sent to 'Nam' earlier, where he had been hit by a grenade, lost both his legs below the knees and taken a lot of shrapnel, much of which was still embedded in his body. Rahula met him in San Francisco, where he had been undergoing operations for several months and been fitted with artificial legs on which he was now learning to walk and make the necessary mental adjustments. When I asked how it felt to visit this terribly handicapped friend he had joined the army with, he said:

"Of course, his spirits were very low. And while I was visiting him and a few other friends that had also been wounded in Vietnam, we got stoned together. It felt a little strange to be with them, imagining what they had gone through and suffered compared with the easygoing times I'd experienced in

Germany. These visits made me reflect on the idea of fate and why people have to experience what they do. What was it that determined my going to Germany and Dave's going to Vietnam and things like that? Could it really be a God that was controlling these life dramas? I really didn't know."

When he told me that, I guessed he might have been very afraid for himself, knowing he was going to that place where all these friends of his had been seriously wounded and asked if it had not crossed his mind to desert.

"No," he said, "for some reason it didn't matter. I accepted it. The only thing I wanted to do was to enjoy the time left to me until I had to leave for Vietnam. But a little later when I went with Dave, who could then get along okay on his new artificial legs, to a big Veterans' Hospital in San Francisco where he had spent several months on his return from Vietnam, I was deeply shocked. He wanted to visit some of his wounded buddies who were still in the hospital.

We went into the large amputee ward where there were about a hundred young men, all of whom had one or two arms or legs missing or a combination thereof. One young man, I observed, had both arms and both legs amputated due to extreme injuries suffered in the war. These wounded people, mostly either sitting in wheelchairs or lying on their beds, were talking or joking amongst themselves.

Some were learning to use their new artificial limbs, and others were quietly reading, sleeping or staring out into blank space. Dave talked with some of the guys he knew while I mostly just hung back. A thought like, 'I may come back like that' entered my mind. After a few minutes of seeing all this, I got butterflies in my stomach and became nauseated. I had to exit quickly to find a bathroom. My body became feverish and I felt very weak. I was amazed at this violent body reaction and patiently waited outside for Dave to come out, after which we left."

This visit occurred while Rahula was trying to enjoy his life as best he could. As he was going to the war in Vietnam and not knowing what to expect, this could, for all he knew, well be the last of the good times for him, and he said: "So I made it count." And what counted was traveling around and getting high on drugs.

In retrospect, for me, it is a peculiar feeling to visualize a young man, surrounded by all of these serious injuries and even death, running with eyes open into his own likely perdition. He was, of course, aware of all the antiwar protests, but he said he did not have any deep emotions about the legality or morality of the Vietnam War and didn't really understand what it was all about anyway. He and all the others were merely told "to stop the spread of evil communism". So it was a kind of unavoidable fate' and he felt he had to tread its path whatever. Luckily, he did not experience any serious trauma in Vietnam.

Chapter 2

"Maybe this world is another planet's Hell," the famous English writer Aldous Huxley once said. It is a very somber perception of life, but a justifiable one, given the nature of the war in Vietnam, which Rahula so fortunately survived. This perception in the light of the beauty of nature and the empathy of love, what some may consider instead as paradise, is a pessimistic view on our life. The concept of *Dukkha* in Buddhist teaching is often criticized as well as pessimistic let alone too pessimistic. That might have its cause in translation. To say life is suffering in general falls as a matter of fact too short of the mark. What suffering in fact means, according to Buddhist teaching, can be explained in the words the historic Buddha himself once used to inform his disciples about it:

"Now this, Bhikkhus, is the noble truth of Dukkha: *birth is* Dukkha, *aging is* Dukkha, *illness is* Dukkha, *death is* Dukkha; *union with what is displeasing is* Dukkha; *separation from what is pleasing is* Dukkha; *not to get what one wants is* Dukkha; *in*

*brief, the five aggregates (*form, sensations, perceptions, mental activity and consciousness) *subject to clinging are* Dukkha.

Leaving behind the cruelty of war does not automatically lead to an understanding of *Dukkha.* Did Rahula appreciate this on returning from Vietnam? As I have already mentioned, anticipating normal, civilian life and escaping from the danger of Vietnam must have been a relief for him after his discharge from the army in January 1971. He said:

"Not only Vietnam, the army as well. I flew from Fort Lewis, Washington, where I was formally discharged from active service, to Los Angeles. At the airport, I quickly went into the restroom, hastily shed my army dress uniform and stuffed it into a trashcan. I put on a pair of faded jeans and tee-shirt, which I had taken with me to Vietnam, got on a bus and headed home to Riverside, thinking: what in God's name is next?"

The next thing turned out to be his re-enrollment at junior college in Riverside (RCC) in order to continue his studies. Nevertheless, apart from anything else, he now began to manifest a slight interest in spiritual matters. At that time, the lives of young people were distinctly characterized by looking at the opportunities that life presented. The whole New Age movement, the reflections of Jesus, the spread of Asian culture was in the air and influenced that generation markedly.

Rahula found he was interested in Transcendental Meditation (TM), which was gaining in popularity. He went with Dave and another friend to the TM lectures that were held at the University of California, Riverside (UCR). He found the lectures well presented and the psychological description of the mental process and different states of consciousness experienced in meditation very interesting. He took the initiation, which also meant having to stop using all non-prescribed drugs. For a period of two weeks prior to the initiation ceremony, he was not supposed to take LSD or smoke pot. He took this as a challenge and stopped using drugs during that period. After initiation, he faithfully began practicing with his mantra, enjoyed the twenty-minute meditations twice a day and felt there was a lot of potential to be developed and value to be had from meditating.

Anyway, that first contact with meditation, even though he liked it, did not change him much. He was more interested in cultivating his hippie image with drug consumption and, after about a month, decided to abandon meditation altogether. However, it did cross his mind that he might come back to it when the desire to get stoned had burned itself out.

The use of drugs was a significant part of his life as it was for the identity of hippie culture generally. The hippie movement had just started in California and spread all over the world; drugs were its elixir. Rahula started consuming them for pleasure, to get high and go the 'whole nine yards'.

Even his time in the army did not change his career as a druggie in the slightest. He told me:

"While in the army, I started to smoke a lot of hashish and took LSD for the first time. Being from California, I was something of a rebel hippie soldier. I had relatively long hair and a moustache and wore 'love beads' and was what the career sergeants and officers called a 'California queer punk'.

During his stay in Germany he often went to Munich with some buddies on the weekends to participate in the carefree hippie scene in the English Garden. And during the summer of 1969, when he only had thirty days left in Europe, he decided to take a quick trip with a friend: two weeks in London and Amsterdam, two cities he had wanted to visit anyway. Besides doing the usual tourist circuit of London, he saw the musical *Hair* and the newly released movie *Easy Rider*. Both of them moved him deeply. In Amsterdam, he reveled in the international hippie drug cult scene, which made the city seem like a 'hippie heaven'. Here he met more young people, as he had done in Munich's English Garden, who told him of their recent adventures traveling overland to India and Nepal. He already felt the nagging desire to travel to Asia one day and the young travelers' tales further increased his desire to go on the same journey.

In the summer break 1971 he took a two-and-a-half month hitchhiking trip through Europe, Spain, and Morocco. In a tiny, nearly deserted Atlantic coastal village, two miles south of the town of Essouira, he met a small group of junkies and one of them reported his adventures traveling across the Middle-East from Istanbul to India, and described all the ins and outs of traveling, all the good dope he had smoked and the wonderful and weird people he had met. These conversations prompted Rahula to decide on definitely planning to travel to India after completing his junior college program.

When registering for the fall semester, he gave up his previous interest in data processing and began taking classes that might be more useful in his future travels. He continued with the Spanish classes he had already begun but also enrolled in classes in cooking, geography, cultural anthropology and world religions. He thought that if he were going to travel halfway around the world to India and possibly beyond, he should have at least a basic working knowledge of the geography, social customs, history and religious beliefs of the countries and peoples he would encounter.

Traveling was a kind of life pursuit anyway. He once told me about the intentions he might have harbored I when he was very young about his future life: "Of course, I had my fantasies, like being in the navy, traveling around and seeing the world. Or maybe like an oceanographer because I was a surfer and I liked the ocean. But all these things were just passing fancies, there was nothing really serious about them. So I didn't really know. And that's one reason why I went on the trip to Asia after my experiences in the army. When I saw how crazy life was and met people from all walks of life and saw the basic struggle to survive up close and conditioned by the places where it occurred, it made me curious. However, I didn't have any concrete ideas about all this and so I said whatever life brings, bring it on."

Here it is, his admirable confidence in life that was already showing when he went to Vietnam despite all the harm that unspeakable war engendered. That confidence in life came with an unquenchable curiosity that might have been indicative of something powerful within him that he was not aware of at the time. Going to India, nevertheless, was for him not merely the hippie's quest for drugs, love and music.

During this time, he came across a copy of *Be Here Now*, the 1971 seminal book by Ram Dass, an American spiritual teacher and writer. He is known for his personal and professional associations with Timothy Leary at Harvard University in the early 1960s and for his travels to India. This book echoes the TM practice of living more or less in the present moment by following the flow of day-to-day situations as they arise. Anyway, it did not force him to follow any rigid pattern of behavior except possibly getting stoned. He thought that living in the present was tantamount to allowing the seemingly automatic course of one's life to take over without trying to control it. So he continued to look around and not be restricted to TM. It was, as he himself put it, like an often unconscious or latent inclination to pull towards truth or God, which is in all of us.

One day, while in Palm Springs, he went inside a huge tent, erected by 'Born again Christians'. He was familiar with the Christian religion from his Sunday school days, and told me he had entered the tent just for the fun of it.

"Once inside the tent," he said, "I listened to a few people relating how they had 'found Christ', how they had been converted to this strong back-to-the-Bible belief. They described how their lives before had been full of confusion and pain, or how they had been addicted to drugs and/or alcohol. But now, they had attained salvation and happiness through a firm conviction that Jesus Christ was the only Son of God and provided the only way to get to Heaven. One of these people came and sat down with me and asked if I believed in God. This was the first time I ever had to think about how to answer this big question."

"Isn't it peculiar," I asked, "considering you had gone to church every given Sunday that, at the age of 23 in a tent in Palm Springs, you were thinking for the first time about whether you believed in God?"

"Yes it is, but I never really had formed a strong conviction or feeling about God or Jesus. I suppose I had more or less just taken them for granted. But now, with my growing exposure to Eastern religion, I was beginning to vaguely relate to that philosophy with its expanded meaning of God rather than to the Christian idea."

"So, how did you respond?"

"I tried explaining to this guy, 'I do not believe God is an individual person or creator or something, who governs the world with an iron fist from his control room in heaven, punishing or rewarding people. God is more like a kind and wise, pervasive energy from which everything has somehow evolved'. That was what I said but truly, I guess, these responses didn't come from any deep personal insight or firm conviction. I was more or less mimicking what I had recently picked up, but it sounded good."

"Sounds good to me as well. What did the born-again-Christian say?"

"This Jesus guy wouldn't buy any of that Eastern way of thinking and he kept interrupting with his witty quotes from the Bible which was supposed to be proof of the Divine law."

In retrospect, you could say that he was on his way—you could discern a certain determination in him, when, in his studies, he came once more into contact with Buddha. A coincidental preparation for this occurred in class when the students were given written assignments concerning the world religions and one of them, in the last semester, was Buddhism, which he therefore studied along with Yoga. When the teacher asked him to write a paper about which religion he liked the most, he chose Buddhism, which prompted him to go to the library. At that time, there were very few books in print on the subject, but he found some and produced the paper.

This was the first time he came into more contact with Buddhist teaching, namely with the concepts of *Karma*, rebirth, suffering, *Nirvana*, and meditation. These Eastern ideas about life, birth and death, even that early in his life, seemed more plausible to him then anything he had heard of before. It was something he could relate to a little better than the standard Judean/Christian philosophy. He said about this paper:

"I had never been so interested and absorbed in writing a school paper and it even surprised me. Now I had a better appreciation and respect for the Buddha statue I still had in my room. I received the highest mark in the entire class, an A-plus, and the teacher wrote praising remarks on my depth of study and comprehension. However, the enthusiasm generated by writing this paper quickly faded away on the conscious level and I was again absorbed in my plans for getting the 'big trip' together."

I wondered about the influence that that very class might have had on him about religions, especially Buddhism. He might not actually have realized it at that time, but he said:

"I don't think that this interest in meditation was motivated by a conscious desire for spiritual enquiry. It was most likely due to a desire to experience something new, which I had always had a penchant for and perhaps my growing disillusionment with being dependent on using dope to get high. Later, on reflection, I realized that it was beginning to knock on doors. The events over the previous years all added their little bit to precipitating this search and would continue to do so, albeit in seemingly odd ways."

When I asked:

"You mean like determined?" he hesitated a bit and said:

"In a sense, yeah, kind of my destiny. I thought that all my former experiences were also a part of it. All the experiences I had had along the way coming from Europe, you know, overland to India was like accumulating the last bit that, when I heard the *Dhamma*, opened up something deeper in me."

The *Dhamma* is the Pali-word for the teaching, the path to enlightenment, and matters in a special way for the concept of Buddhism, because it is one of the 'Triple Gems'. The others are Buddha and *Sangha*. Buddha in this sense is the 'Buddha nature' as the highest spiritual potential that exists within all beings and the *Sangha* means the community of those who have attained enlightenment; it is also used more commonly to refer to the community of practicing Buddhists. The Triple Gem is central to Buddhist thinking and although there is no initiation or any kind of baptism involved in becoming a Buddhist, it is officially considered to be one when one 'takes refuge in the Triple Gem', as it is called.

For Buddhist monks or a follower of the Buddhist teaching, there is no God or creator whatsoever. People unfamiliar with the nature of the teaching might consider, and I have already heard it expressed literally, that Buddha is a God. He is not. He, in one way, is not even a person either, yet, in another way he is: when referring to the historical Buddha, his name is Siddhartha Gautama. He was a human being and did not change himself as such through enlightenment or anything else. He came into his Buddha nature. As a historical figure, he is also called Buddha Shakyamuni because he belonged to the Shakya people. He found enlightenment under the Bodhi tree in Bodh Gaya, a village located in India that, as a result, has become a kind of 'Mecca' for hippies.

Rahula could not really conceal his use of drugs as it was the obvious way of life for a hippie. However, his parents, although they did not approve of it, were aware they could not prevent it. They hoped it might just be a phase their son was going through that would be over sooner or later and, as long as it did not negatively influence his grades, which were above average, they did not consider it important.

In their family, bad problems or tension between its members, hatred or dislike or simply not talking to each other, did not happen. During his childhood, the family travelled around every summer vacation camping and doing other outdoor activities. He was also familiar with nature from having joined the Boy Scouts. He would not call his relationship to his siblings close, but that had mostly to do with their common separation. His sister, five years his senior, had already left the house when she was about eighteen, got married and lived all over other than in California, so he did not see her much. With his brother, a good year older, he would drive to beaches when they were teenagers, and surf together. But later on, he did not have much contact with him either. By the time Rahula had left the army, his brother had also got married, so from then on, it was just him and his parents in their home in Riverside by themselves.

They, of course, hoped he might follow his brother's example, who had never experienced drugs, had a degree in engineering, a well-paid job and had bought a house for his growing family. But Rahula did not intend to obtain a four-year university degree. Two years were enough for him. Only these were not intended to serve any future professional purpose. He supposed he could have become a school teacher or done something with computers because of his earlier start in computer programming. He told me there was a kind of funny side to it all: he started almost at the same time Bill Gates did and, had he finished, he could have been just like BG today!

But he didn't and he isn't: After completing his final exam in good standing for an Associate in Art degree, he did not even wait for the diploma ceremony because that was not as important to him as the immediate pursuit of his desire to travel.

The journey Rahula was so eager to go on, he did not, however, undertake alone. Such was his enthusiasm that he infected three of his pals, old school mates and friends: Barry, Fred and Rick, into going with him. Their slogan was, 'if you're thinking about traveling, then do it'. Nevertheless, while his friends had too much attachment or involvement with jobs, girlfriends or educational pursuits, they agreed just to accompany him as far as Morocco. Hence, they called their forthcoming trip 'The Grand European Expedition'. Rahula might have persuaded his companions with promises of mere fun and adventure, in itself a reasonable enough prospect, however, his own main reason for traveling was for more than just this: he saw it as the opportunity to expand his horizons out of the limitations and routine boredom of working for a living, perhaps in order to give his entire life more meaning.

When I met Barry, a member of his erstwhile travel group, on a trip with Bhante Rahula in California and surrounds, I asked him about what he later thought when he heard his friend wanted to become a monk.

We Rahula and I joined him and a bunch of other friends of his and Rahula's while they were on a camping trip in Joshua Tree National Park. Before replying, Barry emphasized that it was here, in the Park, where he had spent the night when Rahula was ordained. When I wondered how he knew the exact night when it happened, he told me: "We left him, let me think, ..." and Rahula said "'Seventy- three", "yes, in 'Seventy three. I left. Went back to the States; Larry and Rahula went on to Afghanistan. At one point, I realized he was getting more involved with Buddhism and meditation. He was spending more time on retreats, as I gleaned from his letters. I don't remember the first time I saw him after his return, but, yeah, I knew the night of his ordination."

Larry, he mentioned, was his late twin brother, who joined Rahula in Europe and travelled on with him when the others had already gone back. I found it interesting what Barry told me and his joining an old friend mentally on a special occasion seemed very wonderful to me.

"I think we planned it," he continued, "I think I planned it and convinced friends to come out here that night. And to answer your question whether I wondered very much about Rahula becoming a monk. No, not really. Ever since the Canary Islands, he seemed to be gravitating more towards spiritual matters. He spent more time by himself, and I guess it was the beginning of his path into meditation."

That was a hint as to when it started from a friend's point of view. The Canary Islands. Actually Gomera. First of all back then, however, the travellers had to leave the country. They decided on the cheapest and most fun way to reach Europe, which meant driving a delivery car from California to the East Coast. All they had to pay for was the gas. From New York they took a plane to Stockholm and began their 'odyssey' in Scandinavia.

The night before, there was a big going away party in the large house where Barry and Rick were living. Although only old and close friends had been invited, about one hundred people showed up. Ten cases of beer were on hand and steaks were barbecued over a fire pit dug in the back yard. Everyone was drinking beer, smoking hash and grass, nibbling acid and feasting; the music was turned up full blast. The morning after, Rahula said good-bye to his parents, who hoped he would probably become bored or homesick and return to finish his next two years at university. They wished he would return at an appropriate time, although he told them he did not know how long he would be gone for, especially if he discovered something new and interesting enough to keep him; it might be five or ten years before he returned—or perhaps he would never come back.

That was a drastic thing to say and most likely did not sound at all consoling to his parents, and I asked him, if his intention really was to leave for good if the occasion called for it.

"I left," he said, "with the intention maybe never to come back. I didn't have anything to hold me. I mean, I told my parents that, just in case I did find something. And it turned out it was a kind of destiny to find the Dhamma and stay there for five years. There was cause for me to go to India and then there was the effect of being there, which gave me yet another cause."

Chapter 3

Great Expectations is the title of an outstanding novel by the famous English writer, Charles Dickens. Expectations are concomitant with journeys in any case, otherwise nobody would ever go on them. The members of 'The Grand European Expedition' were probably no exception, but considering Rahula's motives, there definitely was something of a great expectation involved, namely the broadening of his mental horizon. An expectation is not an aim, but can be considered as something happening. As it was no great surprise for Barry, at one point, that his friend since seventh grade became a Buddhist monk, so it was not for Rahula either. Expecting to broaden your mental horizon to hardly tells you exactly what will happen. The question is whether it is a deep felt longing or just a passing wish. Anyway, in both cases you have to move.

To attain enlightenment is to move onto the Noble Eightfold Path. If you just have the wish to be enlightened, it will not work. As hard as you might long for it, it is of no avail.

Nirvana, the meaning of being enlightened, is in our 'World of Representation' as unthinkable as something without a beginning or an end. The Noble Eightfold Path, although it is called a Path, has no beginning or end either, hence no direction. The aim in Buddhist teaching and therefore its direction is defined in the fourth of the Noble Truths: to end suffering. I cited the Buddha's definition of suffering in Chapter Two. Here is his definition of the origin of suffering:

Now this, Bhikkhus, is the noble truth of the origin of suffering: it is this craving which leads to re-becoming, accompanied by delight and lust, seeking delight here and there; that is, craving for sensual pleasures, craving for becoming, craving for disbecoming.

Craving not only for physical things, but also for ideas and opinions about ourselves. We grow frustrated when the world around us does not behave the way we would like it to when we are attached to our desires and does not conform to our expectations.

Rahula experienced this in Stockholm, on the first stage of the trip to Europe. One of his expectations was that he could finance the whole trip even as far as India by dealing drugs. Planning a long journey to Europe and Asia one has, of course, to think about the financial issues. The solution to that came through his drug-related contacts, where he found a person who could score four thousand tabs of Orange Sunshine LSD for him.

Each orange capsule was potent enough for four people to get off nicely on, being four-way hits. This was what he wanted to take and sell in Europe to finance his dream, which happened to consist in buying a motorcycle and riding it to India. He paid eight hundred dollars for the whole four thousand, which was actually more than he had planned on, but it was such a good deal, he did not care. He planned to smuggle it into Europe by wrapping the tabs inside his socks at the bottom of his pack.

One reason for choosing Stockholm was because it is situated at the top of the continent and none of the travel group had ever been that far north in Europe; for another, the deciding factor was probably that a good friend of Rahula's knew a dope dealer in Stockholm and he could purchase either all or most of the acid so that he would not have to carry it around everywhere; a third reason was that, during that summer, there happened to be particularly cheap tickets available for Stockholm.

The first thing on the agenda after arriving was to find their Swedish contact. He was a hippie who made jewelry and, with his girl-friend, sold it on the open street-markets. After a little searching, the friends found their apartment and Rahula said:

"When he saw the little orange capsules, his eyes lit up."

He wanted to buy a thousand of them; Rahula had been feeling as if he were sitting on top of dynamite with so many, so this purchase came as something of a relief.

They agreed on a thousand dollars for the deal, money the Swede said he did not have at hand and that it would take him several days to get it, which seemed reasonable to Rahula.

He left the thousand capsules in the Swedish couple's refrigerator and the friends then took off hitchhiking for a week.

Hearing that, I wondered whether stashing it like that had been such a good idea and I said to Rahula:

"You were very trusting and when you came back you realized you shouldn't have left the acid there because the guy was gone and the drugs with him, right?"

"Yes. It was a shock after the nice trip we had just been on. We had gone north, then across to Norway to see some of the fjords, down to Oslo, and then back to Stockholm. The mountain scenery in Norway was spectacular and the fjords and fishing villages were just as I had seen them on postcards. There was nearly 24 hours of daylight this far north, which enabled us to travel virtually all night if we wanted to and still see the countryside."

"But back in Stockholm," I said, "all the nice experiences were gone and you learned how naïve you had been to leave the dope in the possession of someone who was a total stranger to you. Anyway, it could happen just as easily to anyone else. When money is involved, greed arises."

"Yes, I know, but at that time, we were all hippies, hence kind of brothers in pursuit of the peaceful life. However, the girl nervously explained that, the day before, her boyfriend had been peddling some of the LSD in the city square, been arrested by the police and was now in jail. Following up the arrest, detectives came to their apartment to search for more drugs. When they arrived unexpectedly at the door, the girl panicked and quickly flushed all the remaining Orange Sunshine capsules down the toilet."

"But that story, as it turned out, wasn't true, was it?"

"No. When I went down to the city square, where this guy had allegedly been busted in order to think about the whole thing, I saw what I believed to be this same Swedish fellow walking on an overpass above the square. He seemed to see me looking at him and then he quickly ducked out of view. I hurriedly ran up there to try and find him but to no avail. By then, I had a sneaking suspicion that the story, his girlfriend told us was a lie, a cover-up, and called the police to enquire if they had anyone in jail by his name and the reply was negative."

With that, right at the beginning of the big trip, something negative happened, but, fortunately it was the only disturbance for a long time. However, it was clear to Rahula that he would have to give up his dream of buying a motorcycle. Stockholm no longer seemed so nice after that incident and the group headed to Copenhagen, from where one of them, Rick, would be returning home. Rahula recalled his previous visit here in the winter of 1968 while AWOL from the army.

New recruits in every army attend boot camp and advanced training. Afterwards, Rahula, as I have already mentioned, was sent to NATO forces in Germany, where he was assigned to repairing radios on tanks. After six months, he and three friends slipped out of barracks one night, went into nearby Bamberg and got on a train to Copenhagen. After twenty-nine days, they voluntarily returned, were court-martialed and sentenced to three months in an military prison.

Despite this prison experience, by the way, he did it again, when he received notice six month later of his transfer to South Vietnam. He had been given 'two-weeks leave' before having to report to Fort Lewis, Washington from where he would go to Vietnam and he heard that when a person was reporting for duty in Vietnam, they could get away with arriving at Fort Lewis up to one or two weeks late. This was tantamount to being AWOL, but due to the mitigating circumstances—going to Nam was considered thus—generally one did not receive any punishment. For one week of his leave he and a few old friends, including Dave, rented a house on the beach near Ensenada in Baja California, Mexico and partied down just like in the good old days. I wondered about this devil-may-care attitude of his and asked:

"Were there no consequences for you if you were overdue?"

"Not really," he said, "All of us, who were more than three days overdue, and there were many, were given an 'Article 15'. This is the Army's equivalent of a misdemeanor and we were fined twenty dollars for each day we were late. But it was worth while," he confirmed, "even the last day, when we went from the house in Berkeley on an outing to Muir Woods, a protected forest area located north across the Golden Gate Bridge in Marin County. We all ingested some mescaline capsules and spent the afternoon strolling through the tall, thick, shady redwood trees with vibrant green ferns and mosses adding to the luxuriant foliage. I felt very close to this natural beauty and sensed life's subtle energy all around, with the spongy softness of the cool mossy covered earth beneath my bare feet."

His time in Vietnam could be called more or less safe. He was stationed with a medical supply company, where he, due to his college experience with data processing, was selected to operate a stock-record accounting machine processing medical supply orders. It was situated at Long-Binh Post, a large Army base near Saigon, away from active combat zones. Because operating this machine was considered an important job, he was exempt from all other duties and had only to work four or five hours at night in an air-conditioned van especially built to house the delicate electronic system. In January 1971, his three years in the army were over.

After getting home, he received the Army Commendation Medal for meritorious, dedicated service.

"Can you believe it?," he asked me, "I really had to laugh at this because of my previous record of AWOLs, court-martial, prison and using the army as a time to get stoned in almost all the time while seeing so much of the world."

It was indeed amazing. Rahula started smoking marijuana and by and by, he was smoking dope and taking psychedelic drugs because it was the 'in thing' to do. He did not reduce his dope consumption in the army. On the contrary, he increased it while in Germany by smoking a lot of hashish and taking LSD for the first time. In Vietnam he came into contact with heroin. It was easily available in white powder form that he began using by snorting it, but he never put a needle in his arm nor did he get to the point of being uncontrollably addicted. This was what many U.S. soldiers did in order to numb their minds to the horrors and depression of being in a place where they did not want to be. Like the others, he just stayed stoned as much as possible, waiting for the day he would return home.

Copenhagen, the second stage on the Grand European Tour, is a city with a lot of bicycles, already very obvious when you arrive at the main station, where, during the day, commuters park hundreds and hundreds of them. It was already like this in 1972 and attracted Rahula's attention. The idea crossed his mind to ride by bicycle all the way down to Amsterdam, the next major destination. He figured that it would take about ten days cycling through a countryside of mostly very flat farmland and quaint villages to complete the approximately four hundred kilometer journey, but the rest of the guys opted for conventional convenient train travel. The only problem was that taking the bicycles out of the country was not allowed. I guessed he would have considered buying one and selling it later, but he did not, and told this story:

"The rental shops usually did not require any deposit or identification. I guess they figured everyone was honest and the bikes, being so old, no one would want to steal them. Considering these things, it did not take long for me to come up with the idea of renting the bike for a month and just sort of keeping it and riding it down to Amsterdam anyway. I did not think of myself as an out-and-out thief and I justified this devious appropriation by selecting a rusty old girl's bike with bald tires. In my mind it was not worth much more than the one month rental fee I paid for it anyway."

He was probably correct in assuming that the loss to the rental company was insignificant and, sooner or later, that shitty old bike would have had it anyway, but that is not the point. Talking these days about his behavior then, he says:

"On reflection, this was a good example of how the cunning mind and ego can cling to an idea and then outwit or override moral sense."

That is the point and, in comparison, what is the difference between having drugs stolen from him in Stockholm or him stealing a bike in Copenhagen? Neither would qualify as one of the moral disciplinary steps of the Noble Eightfold Path, the Right Action.

Taking what is not given is never right. That step indeed inculcates more, namely the five precepts. These are part of the 'vow' one takes to become a follower of the Buddhist teaching, that is: refuge in the Triple Gems. In that ritual (usually spoken in Pali), one says: "I take refuge in the Buddha, I take refuge in the

Dhamma, I take refuge in the *Sangha*." These form the framework for the transmission of the Buddhist philosophy, and the Five Precepts are regarded as the basic ethical guidelines for the followers of the philosophy, which are: not intentionally killing living beings, taking only what has been given, avoiding sexual misconduct, not speaking falsely, and avoiding intoxicants. Nevertheless, back then, the young Scott could not have cared less about the last item. And the meaning of 'taking only what has been given' can be just as easily expressed as 'not stealing'. Yet, it is broader in its significance for it means developing a sense of fair play and generosity towards others, like, for example, returning borrowed items and not taking unfair advantage.

So, even the excuse he was telling himself that it was not stealing because the bike was not worth more than he paid for the monthly rental rate does not work.

Whatever, the tour with the bike was fun. When he finally got tired of all the pedaling on dirt roads through Northern Germany and Holland, he happily reached Amsterdam with the trusty old bike, where, as planned a few hours after arriving, he met Barry and Fred in the Vondelpark.

"What happened to the bicycle that served you so well?" I asked.

"You'd never guess. I had left it unlocked, leaning against a tree and by the next day it had been appropriated, to be useful to some other person."

The Vondelpark in downtown in Amsterdam was the temporary home for him and hundreds of other transient young hippie travelers from all over the world. His appearance blended right in. The hippie image he cultivated, with his reddish blonde hair hanging below his shoulders and his bushy beard, was supposed to express an independence from societal norms, and served as a visual symbol of the hippies' respect for individual rights. Through their appearance, hippies declared their willingness to question authority.

To me, and not only in retrospect, the hippie era seemed like an attempt to prolong childhood. Most of that generation in the United States, Europe, and Australia did not know what to do but simply did not want to do what their parents did. It was a seeking generation that wanted to live differently. They tried to free themselves from common restrictions and choose their own way to find a new meaning in life. Their lifestyle was characterized by rejecting the so-called establishment, embracing sexual liberation and the use of drugs, and focusing on alternative arts and music. The drugs such as cannabis, LSD, peyote and psilocybin mushrooms were considered to be consciousness expanding. But the consumption of drugs shows that getting permanently high merely induces the desire for more of the same. The fortunate members of this generation realized that getting high was not the solution; those less perceptive turned to hard drugs like heroin, which led to permanent conflicts or worse, namely which ruined everything worthwhile in life. There was nobody that could have known to what group he or she would eventually belong. However, even in that generation, where drug use was very common, it occurred that there were young girls and boys who avoided it or, like me, couldn't stand it. I smoked my first joint, still called at that early time a marihuana-cigarette, and got seriously nauseous. After that, nothing disturbed my intensive sport activities as an athlete or the progress of my education.

That girl I smoked that "cigarette" with and who was already more into the drug scene than I was, started to skip classes to be together with her new drug buddies in bars and cinemas and she later quit the school both of us went to. Fate, for me, is caused by a combination of character, environment and education and you never know, when you are at the beginning of your way, what that combination has in store for you. My only interest, so to speak, in the hippie movement was the rejection of mainstream organized religion in favor of a more personal spiritual experience, often drawing on indigenous and folk beliefs or neo-paganism.

In Amsterdam, Rahula came into contact with Carlos Castaneda's books. Castaneda wrote about his training under the guidance of a shaman called Don Juan Matus. The author describes his personal experiences with peyote and other psychotropic plants, how Don Juan tries to teach him how to use these hallucinogenic substances to unravel the mysteries of the mind in order to develop certain mental powers as an aid to self-realization. Critics have suggested that they are works of fiction; supporters claim the books are either true or at least valuable works of philosophy and descriptions of practices that enable increased awareness. When I read Castaneda's books, I found nice intellectual and metaphysical ideas in them and the experiences described with peyote impressive. I have never had such experiences, because the opportunity has never occurred, but I know that Rahula has and asked him what it was like. He said his use of peyote and magic mushrooms was mostly for the blissful high obtainable and not so much for the deep conscious spiritual discovery that would come only after reading the books. He tried comparing Castaneda's mental experiences with those that he had had when taking mescaline and magic mushrooms, but maintained there was little resemblance. The author's were strong, vivid, and even violent reactions accompanied by doubt and fear, whereas his, said Rahula, were mostly laid back, peaceful, blissful feelings, closely associated with nature.

While in Amsterdam, he also came into contact with Hare Krishna monks. This organization was very well-known to his generation; they too wanted to live differently and often sought aspects of Eastern philosophy and its spiritual concepts in religious and cultural diversity. About the encounter Rahula said:

"I had heard of this controversial group called Krishna Consciousness, but had never seen any of them in person. The Hare Krishna's spiritual guru was a frail old man clothed in pinkish robes and had the traditional ash-colored markings on his forehead. From my study in world religions, I remembered that Krishna was a Hindu god and devotional deity to whom all believers pay homage, and they invoke his blessing by chanting his name, 'Hare Krishna, Hare Rama'. After some introduction, they began chanting the Hare Krishna Maha Mantra with their lively accompanying drumbeat, cymbals and body movement. As the beat picked up, I felt myself being drawn into the rhythm and mood of the chanting. I started silently repeating the words and gradually as I got into it, I chanted audibly. It had a kind of intoxicating, entrancing effect on me and being stoned probably helped to catalyze the whole process. The chanting lasted about fifteen minutes. Much of the crowd had also been drawn into the vibrant mood, swaying and even dancing or jumping up and down along with the monks and devotees. It seemed as though everyone had tuned into the same mental frequency and I felt very high and blissed out. I had heard that devotional chanting of this nature could get a person naturally high. But as I was stoned, I could not be sure if the attraction and good feeling were aroused by the chanting alone or helped along by the dope. A few days later, I went to the Hare Krishna Temple located several blocks away from the Vondelpark. I respectfully observed the proceedings and was surprised when I couldn't help overhearing a few of the monks and devotees quarreling among themselves over some job assignments."

"That was for sure not what you would have expected in a temple…" I interrupted.

"You are right. That did not strike me as proper conduct between spiritual brothers and sisters and especially inside the temple in front of guests. I departed without any strong attraction or positive feelings towards the organized structure and little conviction that this practice was the way to Enlightenment or the realization of God, whatever that meant to me at that time. "

It was in Amsterdam, where the pared down travel group, consisting of Rahula, Barry, and

Fred (Rick, as I have already mentioned, meanwhile having returned due possibly to homesickness), had a vision of the beautiful small island of Gomera in the Canaries; because the summer in Northern Europe would soon be coming to its end, this little group decided to follow the sun and warmth by spending the winter in the Canary Islands.

That, I can tell from my own experience, was a very good idea. The climate is fantastic in winter. Just at this very moment, while writing this, it is December and I am sitting on the veranda of my rented house and observing the ocean glistening in the sunshine out of the corner of my eye. When I heard from Rahula that he too knew the Canaries, we agreed about the magic of the climate. But apart from the wise decision he made to go to Gomera with his friends, he then made another that, as it turned out, was no masterpiece.

Chapter 4

"It is not good that the man should be alone." With those immortal words, written in Genesis, the creator considered the existence of a woman. These words Rahula might have had in mind, when, in Amsterdam, he thought it would not be a bad idea to have a female companion—at least for a while.

What makes human beings unique is, as far as we know, the ability to reflect. We ask, consider, and contemplate on a scale ranging from to simple curiosity to scientific investigation and the question we ask is mostly: 'why?', but it should really be 'what?' or 'how?' because the answer to 'why?' can be easily supplied, namely with the word 'because', which always implies a reason.

The Law of Nature is also a basic idea in *Dhamma* and not understanding the formula of Dependent Arising, as it is called in Buddhism, is considered the root of all sorrows experienced by all beings[1].

In the last chapter, I wrote briefly about why we suffer: we fall prey to longing, aversion, and delusion. If there is a cause, then there is a solution to be found by avoiding the cause. The Buddha said so in the Third of the Four Noble Truths. It is the truth about how we can avoid disappointment, discomfort, anger, sadness, anxiety or suffering.

It happens that meeting a person of the opposite sex sometimes changes his or her life or both lives, sometimes not. Rahula's aim in life was not about becoming a monk back then but traveling and getting to know the world. Sometimes being accompanied by a woman could promise more fun, but he was not interested in the slightest in a serious relationship. In Amsterdam, he decided to invite Gail, a former girlfriend from Riverside, to come over and join him to travel to the Canary Islands. He guessed it was because he had made enough money and could afford to buy her a round trip ticket, but he did not have the intention of taking her to India. He said:

"I suppose, remembering the previous summer's

---

1 The principle of dependent arising doctrine in Buddhism (Pratityasamutpada) describes the chain of causes which result in rebirth and suffering. Everything except Nirvana is conditioned by Pratityasamutpada.

experience with Terri, I also missed a female's tender touch and desired a companion to accompany me while hitchhiking south."

He had met Terri in Amsterdam. She was from Santa Cruz and hitchhiked with Rahula down to Spain. It is pretty obvious that remembering being with her led to his present decision because with her it was like reliving the hippie era of free love. They travelled through Germany and Southern France, visited Pamplona in Spain at the time of the 'running of the bulls' festival, continued down to Barcelona, from where they cruised to Ibiza. This beautiful little Balearic island was famous for offering the liberty of a hippie way of life on its myriad beaches. He spent five very restful, enjoyable days with Terri on an uncrowded beach drinking wine, smoking hash, sun-tanning in the nude and making love in the moonlight. When Rahula continued his journey down to Morocco, Terri was due to head back to college in California. He describes the time with her as 'a pleasurable, casual relationship without attachment'. When they parted, there was no regret, ill feeling or guilt. With the memory of this very comfortable and free relationship in mind, he asked Gail to join him.

Gail and Rahula used to go to the same Spanish class. Although this girl was only nineteen, she already had a three-year old daughter. A case of the common teenage 'puppy love' affair and sexual promiscuity which flourished then in American society and ended with many unwed mothers. The father of the child was living in another town. They were never married and so Gail was living alone with her daughter. She had to hire a babysitter to take care of the child while she was at college or working her part-time job. Two days a week she and Rahula had class together and he stayed at her house the previous night and in the mornings they went to school together.

When he told me about it, I guessed it was not a serious relationship and asked:

"It obviously didn't have influence enough to change your plan to go on the big journey, did it?"

"No, it wouldn't have been in any case, but anyway, after a while she began developing more attachment and possessiveness towards me than I could handle. At school, she always wanted to be with me, to hold hands and so on. I felt uncomfortable in this situation, probably because of my previous liberal experience with Terri and the freedom I had enjoyed. It also cut into the amount of time I was spending with the guys. I still wanted to be free to go out with my friends to get loaded, drink beer, go to parties and so on. But at the same time, I wanted to have a woman whom I could enjoy sexually. I guess, I was not ready for a serious, personal love relationship with one person, where I would have to exercise so-called adult or mature responsibility. Nevertheless, we continued our relationship, but I made it clear to her that I would be going on an unlimited, unconditional trip to India in a few months' time. For all intents and purposes, that meant terminating our close relationship."

And it did. On the driveway of his house in Riverside, where he made his farewell to his parents, there was also a sobbing Gail saying good-bye with hugs and kisses.

To his big surprise, it was a different Gail than Rahula had expected that arrived in Amsterdam. She declared directly she arrived that she no longer felt motivated to have an intimate, sexual type of relationship with him because she felt deeply hurt after he had abandoned her. Now her feelings had changed. She wanted just to be friends, traveling companions. Rahula was dumbfounded.

"I had been without extended female companionship for over two months," he said "and was more or less looking forward to Gail's previous sexual submissiveness."

"Hard luck, to put it simply," I said.

"Yes, and I on the first night in the park together, encountered her reluctance and coldness towards sex, and suffered a lot. It was mostly fostered by my expectations, attachment and unwillingness to accept her independence and change of attitude: a good example of what causes suffering, outlined in the Second Noble Truth as craving."

Anyway, Gail was present and part of the group on Gomera, where, for the first two days, they camped among some bushes by the seaside near a village with a string of houses, restaurants, bars and a few small hotels. Then they looked for and found a nice large house near the beach. The landlord was the owner of a cantina where they went nearly every night to drink beer, often getting quite drunk. A month after their arrival, Rahula decided to move up into the rear of the valley and live alone. He wanted to get out of that heavy partying atmosphere and also away from Gail. He found a place situated high up in the valley. On top of the bedroom was a sunroof, which afforded a majestic view down the whole length of the valley to the beach about five miles away. It was here that Barry was wondering about his old friend's behavior in retreating from the group and, as he told me much later, that he little knew Rahula was on a different path.

In that sanctuary, Rahula lived with an old man and his fragile wife in a stone hut directly in the back. They were very poor but had a big pig they were fattening up for the winter. The pigpen was just a few feet from the edge of the sunroof. The 'old porker', as Rahula called it, used to snort and grunt a lot as if trying to tell him something. He grew fond of the hog and called it Petunia. When they slaughtered it, he was saddened. It made him reflect on fate and how each living creature, including mankind, is affected by its surroundings.

In time he got to know most of the villagers and became good friends with many of them. By socializing like this, he was able to improve his Spanish, and the locals were delighted. A few of the men, who had problems pronouncing the name Scott, started calling him *El Rubio*, 'the fair-haired'. One man liked him so much that he wanted Rahula to marry his daughter and stay there on the mountainside in an extra family house.

"It sounds like a tempting offer," I said and he replied:

"Yes, but I was not quite ready for such a move. On the other hand, there was Gail and, after three weeks of separation, I asked her if she would like to move in with me up there. I thought maybe our relationship might improve in those changed surroundings. I had done a lot of serious thinking and realized that it was my possessiveness and sexual attachment which was the major cause of her alienation from me and I hoped to rectify it. I had come to understand something about the nature of lust and what a strong and unpredictable force it can be. Gail, however, had, in the weeks of separation, met many other people and was enjoying her freedom."

"So, there obviously was no happy ending with Gail. Mightn't your journey and life have otherwise taken another direction? "

"I don't know, but even I couldn't help, from time to time, mulling over the whole situation—after finally accepting the fact that our intimate relationship was over—I, nevertheless, wouldn't have invited her on the next trip. Both of us had discussed leaving Gomera for Morocco a lot. She wanted to join me, but didn't have enough money and I had stopped supporting her financially after she had refused to come to stay with me. Anyway, about all the money she had left was just enough for her to take the ship back to Spain and the train up to Amsterdam, where she could fly back on her still valid return ticket."

"Did she do as you expected and go back to California?", I asked.

"Back then, she did not tell me exactly what she would do, except that, for the time being, she would remain at the house of some friends. About seven months later, when I was in Athens, I bumped into a German who had just returned from Gomera. He told me that Gail had since gotten herself pregnant by a local resident, whom I had also known well, and she was now married to him. That shocked me somewhat and I thought, 'that was real quick work!'."

Going to Morocco was, from the beginning,

part of the plan because of the experiences he had had on the trip a year before. So, all of the 'Riverside Gang' were going. Rick, who left in Copenhagen, was, as previously mentioned, replaced on the Canary Islands by Barry's twin brother, Larry.

They cruised on an old steamer with a lot of other young western travelers on the 'hippie trail', following the seasons from one paradise to another. Before arriving in Marrakesh, which was a focal point or 'Mecca' on the Moroccan hippie trail, they spent some time in the countryside. There it happened again that, at a nomadic tent area, some Berber offered Rahula his daughter in marriage. Again he declined, politely but steadily, as he told me, and added:

"But not without images flashing through my mind of spending a life ever after in the Sahara, tending goats and drinking mint tea."

Cheap hotels in Marrakesh, the local delicacy—large potent hash cookies made at the bakery and available in certain teashops—bizarre and wonderful markets featuring hundreds of hawkers selling all manner of local and imported goods, along with musicians, snake charmers, dancers, colorfully dressed water vendors with their giant leather water bags, and a plethora of mouthwatering food stalls were a paradise for the visitors. Nevertheless Barry and Fred decided they had had enough of travelling. They, in the first place, did not want to go to India with Rahula anyway. So now it was just him and Larry, who wanted to stick it out with him at least as far as Afghanistan. Both of them continued to Algeria, from where they flew to Palermo in Italy and caught a boat to Athens at Brindisi.

Young Scott DuPrez travelled straight to the fate destined for him, although there were seemingly some detours, but I do not think you can really call them that. It is common for young people to be curious about life and the world. In his generation, maybe the first in history, a lot of young people left their home countries to explore the outside world and foreign cultures. After a while, most of them returned, like his companions, and continued their interrupted education or started a job. However, that was not to be his destiny and little did Rahula know this at the time as can be understood from his reply to his mother when she asked him when he would return.

He said he did not know. That was because he might, as he put it, "discover something new and interesting enough that will keep me there".

In that case it could be five or ten years before his return or perhaps he would never come back. It was in line with his earlier thoughts about what he might be doing as a grown up, namely joining the Navy to travel around and see the world. The alternative, becoming an oceanographer, also shows that he did not feel cut out for staying at home. Coming to Athens was part of his eager pursuit to reach this 'something'. It seems he had the so-called 'travel gene' or, as his mother told me when I was sitting with her and Rahula in her home in Riverside:

"He's always had the wanderlust. He likes to go to different countries. But I did too. He got that from me …" and Rahula said:

"Yes, that's true, I got it from her."

Everybody has inside of him- or herself a feeling of strangeness: something we do not know. When it comes to facing it, there are two options, namely refusing it or going along with it. If you go along with it, it means it will not longer be strange, it becomes part of your life, broadens your horizon, opens your mind. Everything in it seems to change your life. Even a tiny part might have a huge impact. But judgment, whether tiny or huge, is only in the eye of the beholder. For one's own destiny, however, it does not matter because every step is the same for everyone and in a way determined. Even in the case of committing crimes. For that there are consequences and not just in the penalties incurred if caught in the act, but also in one's behavior, feelings, and actions afterwards.

What Rahula did in Afghanistan was, for one thing, what brought him back to Athens instead of going straight to India via Pakistan and for another, made his loving parents suffer—parents, it seems, who were understanding, caring, demanding no more than was needed, and providing him with a childhood free of care. Their son's drug abuse was a challenge they shared with a lot of other parents at that time and I guess they could not imagine how excessive it was. The first time they might have had an inkling was when they got to know that he, while serving the army, had been court-martialed and sentenced to three months in a military prison back then in Germany.

His parents' initial reactions were of disbelief, horror and shock. These feelings were, however, to be greatly amplified by what came to pass in Afghanistan.

From Athens, where he and Larry spent a week waiting for the visa for Iran, they left for the Greek island of Rhodes, from where they crossed the Aegean Sea to Marmara in Turkey and reached Afghanistan by train and bus. In Herat, a city near the border, Larry and Rahula spent three days acclimatizing to the noticeable contrast in culture and personality and headed then to Kandahar, a small, pleasant, city in the southern desert where for two weeks they rented a cheap hotel room and bicycles for riding out on to peaceful spots where they could go swimming, sunbathing, picnicking, take naps and, of course, get stoned.

Drug users not only have to be on their guard when crossing borders, but also have to reckon on the possibility of getting caught within them. Considering the permanent danger the situation presented, it is not easy to understand what possessed both of them to do what they did, when they came to leave Kandahar for Pakistan.

Out of their many contacts in Kandahar they met a man who had a hemp farm and hash factory. At that time, Larry had definitely decided to return home.

Rahula, however, wanted to go via India up into the Himalayas. He knew that hash was cheaply available in Pakistan, India and Nepal. Nevertheless, he wanted to have the best, the 'number one' Afghani, something to be one up about and coveted by the rest of the western freaks.

So he decided to take a kilo of the best quality Afghani hash to India with him. Larry also decided to risk taking two hundred grams back with him. In Pakistan, he would then head west across the southern part of the country and continue via Iran back to Athens. Rahula on the other hand would travel up to Lahore, cross the border near Amritsar into India, and head up into the Himalayas, where, in accordance with his fantasy, he would find a quiet, amenable, picturesque spot and just stay stoned as long as it lasted.

When I talked to him about the risk that could come with smuggling drugs and whether he had not thought about it, he said:

"In our talks with the dealer, he assured us he had helped many tourists sneak hash out of the country and suggested a fool-proof way to smuggle the dope across the border. He would have half a kilo sewn neatly into an afghan vest to be confidently worn undetected through customs. This method, he boasted, had worked many times.

"I decided to sew the other five hundred grams into the flat bottom of my knapsack, while Larry was going to take his two hundred grams strapped over his crotch."

It turned out that the whole plan proved to be a stupid idea when the bus they were riding arrived at the border. It was around noon and very hot, which caused the hash in the vest to heat up and give off a subtle odor. When they realized this, the bus was already pulling up at the Afghan customs' checkpoint. Rahula told me what happened next:

"The bus stopped and Larry and I, being the only foreigners, were ordered to get out and report to the customs building with our luggage. We were ushered into the inspection room where four customs officers were casually waiting. The first thing one of them asked rather frankly and routinely was, 'Do you have any hashish?' Such a quick, direct and accurate question caught us off guard and we didn't know which of us should respond. I was more or less speechless and sensing this, Larry promptly replied in the calmest, most convincing manner possible, 'No sir, we do not use drugs, we just want to go to Pakistan.' Evidently the chief inspector was not convinced of this lie and, not wanting to beat around the bush, he started searching Larry beginning with his small pack. Failing to find anything in Larry's pack, the officer began searching his body. All the while, Larry was trying to divert the inspector's attention by talking casually about the weather, etcetera. The inspector, however, was not sidetracked by this small talk and continued to search, striking alarmingly closer to home. It seemed as if he were deliberately leaving Larry's crotch till last, and Larry was beginning to jubilantly imagine that he would make it. After a slight hesitation, the officer turned around and put his hand firmly onto Larry's private parts. His eyes lit up at the surety of his find, he announced 'Hashish!', and our hearts sank. I knew I was next and the butterflies in my stomach were overpowering. The inspector then turned to me while sniffing the air and, within a matter of minutes, found the hash in the vest followed by the stash at the bottom of my pack. The escapade was over; we were caught red-handed, busted big time."

The consequences of the incident at the

Afghan border were, as a matter of fact, not that bad. Compared with the horror scenarios they had heard before of Turkish and Iranian prisons, where foreigners sometimes spent years on similar charges in a much filthier and more dismal environment, their time in the Afghan prison was more like a holiday. Bearing the 1978 American movie *Midnight Express* in mind, which was based on an incident at Istanbul Airport in 1970 in which an American was caught with two kilos of hashish and suffered serious torture in prison, one can say that Larry and Rahula were very lucky indeed.

They were brought into the "little jail", as it was called. The first thing both of them noticed was a group of men standing under the shade of the only tree, hacking and coughing, the old familiar sound of hookah smoking, and a voluminous cloud of smoke above their heads. They beckoned Rahula and Larry to come over for a blow on the big hookah.

The jail was a square, roofless, dirt floor compound formed by the high mud wall with a double strand of drooping, rusty barbwire running along the top. The rooms, each for about ten men, were located along the perimeter. An open, foul-smelling latrine area was situated in one corner, while a nice, clean bathing room with a deep, fresh-water well graced the center of the courtyard. Prisoners had to bring their own bedding, usually a straw mat and a blanket, their own cooking utensils, and to arrange for food to be brought from outside.

Luckily they were permitted to keep enough money so that they could pay a willing guard to go to the market to purchase food or other personal articles for them.

The big hookah was left most of the time underneath the big shady tree and Rahula and Larry used it on a few occasions, but enjoyed their own Moroccan pipes, a chillum, or made themselves joints most of the time. So they spent those two weeks in a pretty wasted state, which, however, proved helpful in alleviating an intestinal disorder they attributed to the greasy mutton stew they were eating.

Concerning the subsequent trial, this is what Rahula had to say:

"Larry and I were marched across town to the courthouse buildings situated in the middle of a huge park with many trees. The courtroom where we were to be tried was on the second floor of this three-story building. In the courtroom the judge, an elegant looking old gentleman with a white beard and turban, was sitting on a raised platform in a big chair. The two of us were instructed to sit on the carpeted floor in front. Ours was clearly an open and shut case. We were admittedly guilty in the first degree. I was fined five hundred U.S. dollars and Larry two hundred. Fortunately we had the money to pay the fines. If not, it would have meant an indefinite amount of time in jail until the fine was paid."

After their release, Larry had only enough money to make it back to Madrid for his return flight. Rahula decided to return with him to Athens, as it seemed to be the safest place to receive money from the United States.

Rahula wrote to his parents, truthfully relating the reason for his and Larry's recent arrest and imprisonment and asked for 500 Dollars to be wired from his account to the Bank of America in Athens. It might be embarrassing to describe experiences such as these, but that was nothing compared with what the next 'exploit' would bring.

Getting busted was apparently not a strong enough deterrent to rid them of their greed because the unlucky pair subsequently forged a plan to make a little extra money for the trip back to Athens. At that time, it was a popular scam to sell one's unsigned travelers' checks to a dealer for half their value, then declare the checks stolen by reporting the 'theft' to the funding agency in order to receive a full reimbursement. Larry did this with his remaining fifty dollar check, but Rahula was contemplating another way because he had previously cashed a check while the clerk did not even check his passport or even bother to watch him sign. So, ruled by his greedy mind (his own expression), he had Larry forge his signature on a one hundred-dollar check prior to entering the bank. The clerk, as before, neither asked for his passport nor did he watch him sign. Later, they then reported their respective travelers' checks as stolen and, went immediately to the American Express office on reaching Teheran and, within two hours, received their refunds without difficulty.

In Istanbul they parted company. Rahula decided to travel through the Greek Islands for about two weeks, waiting for his money to arrive at the bank in Athens. When back in Athens, he found a letter from his parents. He did not feel comfortable opening it, being mindful of his confession to them about his prison time in Afghanistan. What else could he expect other than reproaches or, worse: that they would refuse to send his money because they wanted him to come home. As it happened, he would have had no alternative then but to return to Riverside, come to his senses and maybe finish his last two years of college.

What he read in that letter, however, was worse than anything he could have imagined. The sermon he had been expecting from his parents about his time in jail was in the letter of course. They were surprised that he had got off so easily, having read the stories being published in the newspapers about Americans in Turkish and Iranian prisons on dope charges plus the generally long and severe punishments meted out to them, and they were really glad that everything had worked out so well for their son, but after expressing that, they dropped the bomb: they had received a shocking letter from the American Express Company headquarters stating that their son had tried to swindle them out of one hundred dollars. For some reason the AMEX central office did not believe Rahula's story and accused him of fraud. They demanded that either the money be repaid or he be taken to court. His parents, not really knowing exactly what had happened, quickly pacified AMEX by sending the money.

Rahula not only admitted the fraud to himself openly right away when he read the letter, but also later affirmed this situation with some compassion:

"With these two seemingly terrible criminal blunders coming so close together, my parents were deeply disturbed. They felt I must have entirely lost all sense of right and wrong, shame and reason, and had stooped to the lowest of the low. They were immensely disappointed in, confused by and ashamed of me and they certainly did not tell anyone else, as they had about my other unlawful adventures. However, mom did wire my money, which arrived a few days later."

It is pretty obvious the actions produced mental anguish in at least two parties, and, as described earlier, it is proof, of what the Second of the Four Noble Truths implies, namely that one of the causes of mental anguish is greed. However, it can be pointed out that if Rahula had not been caught at the border and AMEX had not discovered the fraud, there would have been no problem. Hence the cause of suffering in this case might not have been greed so much as the fact of getting caught. Nevertheless that point of view misses the fact that every action influences its perpetrator. Some call it having a guilty conscience. However, it is part of your feeling, who you are.

Rahula's character, which, as it turned out later, had the potential to find Right Understanding in the meaning of Buddhist teaching, also clearly had the potential to commit crime. In addition to the two incidents that came up in his parent's letter, there was a third he later mentioned to me:

„Before that, I'd stolen a turquoise stone in a shop with my friend," and than added, " if I'd got caught, they would have cut my hands off maybe."

That could have been in Iran, where he and Larry, among other tourists, visited a turquoise factory where they bought some stones for drug-dealing purposes or to bring them home as gifts. They each stole an extra stone, independently of each other, and had a laugh about it later when they realized they had both had the same idea.

The Four Noble Truths can be described in four words: diagnosis, cause, recovery, treatment. The diagnosis implies that life inevitably involves some mental and physical anguish, the cause of which is ignorance and craving; the recovery from it is the attainment of enlightenment, which is achieved through a form of gradual training: the treatment, the Noble Eightfold Path. Mental and physical pain is considered to be what everyone at some point experiences: disappointment, discomfort, anger, sadness, anxiety or suffering; not always getting what is wanted and often being separated from whom or what is loved. Furthermore, the gradual physical degeneration of old age can be difficult and, in any case, every life ends in death. Ignorance and craving cause the longing for sensual pleasure, the clinging to aversion and a deluded perception of reality.

Part of the treatment, the Noble Eightfold Path, is *Sila*[2] (Ethical Conduct) with its three steps: Right Speech, Right Action, Right Livelihood. It is a concept of the Buddhist Teaching, simply put, that everything you are when doing wrong causes a lack of peace of mind,

2   *Sila* (virtue, morality) is one of the three practice foundations in Buddhism and considered a "great gift" (*Mahadana*) to others, because it creates an atmosphere of trust, respect, and security. This is virtue, or moral conduct. It consists of right speech, right action and right livelihood

which is the aim as stated by the historical Buddha: to be free of suffering.

Anyway, the suffering caused by his behavior in Afghanistan was obvious and did not just involve Rahula. Both incidents (or actually three) not only originated in his desire to get high on drugs but also in his greed for financial gain and could have jeopardized his life by turning it in a very bad direction indeed. But they did not. Rahula described his emotions after reading the letter:

"Now that everything was out in the open concerning those two events, the guilt and worry that I had been carrying around in my mind and even to a certain extent in my body were largely dissipated and I felt much better. It was now a matter of resolving not to undertake such foolhardy illegal stunts in the future, which would jeopardize my freedom and wellbeing and, at the same time, cause my parents mental turmoil. As they had with my court-martial in the army, I figured my parents' despair and grief would eventually subside and the events would, in time, be as good as forgotten."

After a full year and two months since he had left the USA, he finally entered India. On his way from Athens, he crossed the Afghan border exactly where he had been arrested three months before.

India was at that time the hippies' promised

land, that most paradisiac place, and his destination was Goa, which actually did not belong to the state of India at that time, but happened to be a Portuguese colony.

In India, he spent his first night at the Golden Temple of Amritsar. It is the holiest of the holy places for Indian Sikhs and, more or less, the center of the Sikh religion. It could be compared to Mecca for the Muslims, the Vatican for Catholics, Jerusalem for the Jews and the Bodhi Tree in Bodh Gaya for Buddhists.

Chapter 5

Three Wayfarers sat down at nightfall and started a card game. The youngest, free of care, put his card on the table and claimed to have the best one because it represented Happiness. The second, with his pale rutted face, was not impressed and told the youngster not to brag so much, arguing his card was higher because it represented Pain. Whereupon the third gave only a gloomy laugh and when he displayed his card, they saw it stood for Death.

This is a short summary of a poem by the German poet Carl Busse (1872-1918). But is death really the trump card? What is afterlife or rebirth? These concepts are often merely considered as comforts for those people (perhaps all of us) who fear that death is final. Maybe that is their point, but the term 'rebirth', at least in Buddhist teaching, does not entail relief, nor is it limited to 'reincarnation'. The historical Buddha pointed out that he understood rebirth to be an impersonal causal process in which all physical and mental phenomena always require subsequent physical and mental phenomena. The relationship between cause and effect within this entire, impersonal causal process is such that cause and effect are neither identical nor different, so there can be no consolidation because there is no "substance" or "soul" that can remain the same, immortal to itself.

There is another central aspect: rebirth in early Buddhism had an elemental meaning related to this world. The standard statements in the ancient speeches on liberating insights, which imply the realization of *Nirvana*, clearly show that *Samsara*[3] is finally complete at the time of these liberating insights into life. *Samsara*, the cycle of repeated reincarnation, is immanent to existence!

Nirvana is the state of mind that has become free from the delusion and separateness of the ego, free therefore from greed, hatred and delusion, and its basis is the liberation from the ego and all its connections including suffering. Rahula said in this context: "But there is still awareness and so on, but of a different kind. It's the natural state of pure mind. The word *Nirvana* actually means 'going out of craving' and, although it is the deepest level of understanding, the mind can not immediately

3   *Samsara* in Buddhism is the endless cycle of birth, rebirth, and re-death without beginning or end. The Four Noble Truths are aimed at ending this cycles associated as suffering. The liberation is Nirvana.

experience it. The ego and other things prevent its full realization and allow only a brief glimpse of it."

Nevertheless, *Nirvana* can be realized here and now in life. The 'cycle of existence' primarily means these constant little 'births', this 'getting old again and again' of things when they fade away, as well as this 'dying again and again' when they cease. This is the significance of the 'cycle of reincarnation' with its suffering caused by the lack of liberating insight.

The deeper the insight, the less the suffering. The more insight is realized, the more deeply sympathetic, loving and compassionate towards people, animals and the world we become because we no longer suffer from a feeling of impermanence. If it is deeply understood that it makes no sense to cling to impermanent things and sensations, then pain and suffering will cease. This leads to the 'definitive liberation' in life, to *Nirvana*, and implies that there is no longer any continued existence after physical death.

On Rahula's journey through India from Delhi, which he visited to get a visa for the trip to Nepal, he stopped in Agra to see the Taj Mahal, and then traveled by train eastward to Varanasi, the major religious heart of India. It is the holiest of the seven cities sacred to Hindus and Jainists. It is also considered to be important in the historical development of Buddhism. The city is located along the west bank of the River Ganges, the river also sacred to the Hindus. Believers come from all over India to bathe in the water, which is thought to be blessed with special purifying qualities. When a Hindu dies, it is auspicious to have the corpse soaked in the river before cremating it. Right by the riverbank are the burning Ghats, where, from early morning to late into the night, approximately a hundred or more bodies are cremated every day.

Rahula spent some time observing the cremations. When he was a kid, he sometimes lay in bed at night before falling asleep, trying to imagine what it would be like to die. For him, the idea of never being able then to experience the human world as we know it was a little scary.

I guess it is a common reaction when we come to think about death. Psychological studies even indicate that the fear of death for human beings is a basic anxiety. Some, I know from my own observations, say that they do not want to hear or talk about it. That might imply that they deny thinking about it as well. I believe this is a pity, since to understand the reality of life implies the obvious fact of death. It is a remarkable fact that Rahula, who was always eager to get high, became aware of the true nature of the reality of life when he thought about death. It was also one of the main issues at the very beginning of his spiritual development and an essential gateway to

'Right Understanding', when he observed the bodies burning up, going from life to ashes in a matter of hours. He pondered the reason for birth and death and the insignificance of the physical body in the wake of death with the immediate onset of decomposition. This insight, at the burning Ghats in Varanasi, might have set the cornerstone for him to the foundation of 'Right Understanding' in the sense of the Buddhist concept as a step on the Noble Eightfold Path, which meant seeing the world not as he believed or wanted it to be, but as it really is.

Nevertheless, he was still as far away from Buddhist teaching as he was before. No matter, he was acquiring his first religious label in the form of a lightweight shawl decorated with different combinations of Hindu and Buddhist symbols and mantras. He said about this:

"I had just seen a number of Westerners with these and desired to have one for myself to look quasi spiritual. After meticulously searching through piles and boxes of shawls trying to make up what color and design combination I wanted, I finally selected a light yellow color dotted with the Sanskrit letter for OM and images of a seated Buddha. I used to wear it draped around my shoulders, copying others, and occasionally used it as a headband to tie back my lengthening hair."

Further along his way, he arrived in Pokhara,

a mountain village at the end of a large, long valley. From here he had his first impression of the Himalayas, with a impressive view of the surrounding mighty peaks. And here it was that he and his traveling companion, Ronald, who he first met in Afghanistan and again later on his way through India, started a trek into the mountains. This 'round trip to Jomsom' usually takes about ten days for its more than one hundred miles. After resting at the first stop, Ronald, who had not been feeling well towards the end of the trip the day before, was feeling no better in the morning.

Rahula, who fancied dropping some acid and tripping in the Himalayas under the waning half moon, tried to wake Roland early at 4:40 am, who replied that he would have to stay back to get more sleep and rest. For Rahula, it seems the tempting clear sky with the half-waning moon lighting up the mountain peaks was a once-in-a-lifetime occasion. So he did not mind when Ronald told him to take off without him and that he would try and catch up with him later in the day. Rahula said he would wait in the next major village, then took some LSD and went off.

At the next major village, he waited for about five hours. From a few trekkers he then got news about his companion. Rahula already had a vague suspicion that Ronald was possibly coming down with hepatitis. However, his plan came first, so he brushed the threatening intrusion out of his mind immediately. As it turned out, his guess was correct. Ronald had to return to Pokhara, where he would stay in the hotel and recover. This news caused Rahula a bit of irritation and he thought about turning back, but finally decided to continue the trek.

During his walk that day, he felt guilty at having left Ronald behind. Now these thoughts continued and mingled with what had happened in Manali when Rahula was down with the same disease and it was Ron who had helped and cared for him. Deep down Rahula knew that he should have returned, even if just to give Ron moral support and be there; someone for him to talk to. Later Ronald said, when they accidentally met again:

"I thought we were friends, but what are friends for if not to stick around and help out in such situations?"

And he reminded Rahula that he had stuck by him, when sick, until he was on his feet again and guessed that he had probably contracted the germ from Rahula while taking care of him.

It was not a nice situation. Not for Ronald in his sick condition and neither for Rahula with his guilty conscience. But leaving his friend in an uncomfortable situation implied not only a very possibly mean and selfish form of behavior, but was also significant in a way. Not in that fatalistic sense, where it does not matter what you do because anything will lead you to the same, predetermined result, but in the sense that whatever you do will lead to a certain, predetermined result because the 'movement' of the cause is unstoppable until a stopping action occurs. Like a ball on the top of a hill which, once set in motion, will roll down and come to rest at a place predetermined by the slope and the surface of the ground. At the outset, nobody can figure out easily where that place might exactly be, yet the only way the ball will not reach its predetermined destination is through the intervention of another action, for example, the ball is suddenly kicked in a different direction. Conditioning for life is determined in general by different phenomena such as genes, education, environment etc. and in detail by greed, hatred and delusion. A man greedy enough to 'walk under a waning half moon' rather than care for a friend makes this decision out of those conditional basics and will continue to do so. On his way, he will experience what lies ahead and he will be confronted by the mental anguish caused by his greedy mind, although he has no choice in the matter. The potential for staying with and caring for a friend are indeed within him as well, but he does not stay because the conditions call for him to move on.

Two days later, he met a young Englishman,

called Jim, who had been in India a while before coming to Nepal. Rahula recalled this situation:

"After exchanging the usual polite traveler's talk, the guy began talking about an experience at a ten-day meditation course in India he had just finished. At this point, I became more attentive and listened with interest as he explained in detail about this certain meditation practice, which is called *Vipassana*. It involves concentrating the mind inside the body and systematically becoming aware of the different sensations that occur. He described the process in such vivid detail that I became intrigued and absorbed. He said after the first five days of the meditation course, when his concentration had greatly improved, he began feeling increasingly subtler sensations, what he called body vibrations, coming and going or arising and vanishing. He could not explain too well, as he said the experience was difficult to put into words. Every night during the ten-day course, the teacher, a Burmese man named Goenka, gave a talk on some aspects of Buddhism, or *Dhamma* as he called it, with the emphasis on the idea of universal impermanence and Buddha's Four Noble Truths."

Rahula was very impressed by Jim's account and wanted to join this meditation course. But had no desire to return to India that early. Then Jim added that a one-month course in

Tibetan meditation would be starting in about three weeks' time in Katmandu. While he had never taken it himself, he knew that the teachers were two Tibetan Lamas, who spoke acceptable English and had been teaching Tibetan Buddhist meditation to Westerners for the previous five years. They had many devoted western followers including several who had become monks and nuns. These courses were considered a very influential introduction to *Mahayana* Buddhism with a potentially transforming affect on the lives of those participants who completed the training.

This was the first time that Rahula had heard the word '*Mahayana*'. This term is the name of one of the two or three (depending on one's point of view) different schools of Buddhism: *Theravada, Mahayana,* and *Vajrayana.* The last is sometimes classified as a part of *Mahayana.*

Theravada admits the human characteristics of the Buddha and is characterized by a psychological understanding of human nature. It emphasizes a meditative approach to the transformation of consciousness. The teaching of the Buddha, according to this school, is very plain: the development of ethical conduct, meditation and the wisdom of insight (*Sila, Samadhi, Pajna*). This philosophy states that all worldly phenomena are subject to three characteristics—impermanence, suffering and non-self (*Anicca, Dukkha and Anatta*). When the perfected state of insight (wisdom),

Nirvana, is attained, that person becomes an *Arahant,* which means 'one who is worthy' or a 'worthy person'. The life of the *Arahant,* as the ideal of the followers of *Theravada,* is a life where all (future) births are at an end, where the holy life is fully achieved, where all that has to be done has been done, and there is no more returning to the worldly life, to the *Samsara.*

In *Mahayana,* the Buddha is seen as the ultimate, highest being, present at all times, in all beings, in all places and connected only externally with worldly life. The ideal of the *Mahayana* school is to become a Bodhisattva, a person representing the universal ideal of altruistic excellence, delaying his or her own enlightenment in order to compassionately assist all other beings.

Vajrayana, predominant in the Himalayan nations like Tibet and Nepal, is esoteric in the sense that the transmission of certain teachings only occurs directly from teacher to student intuitively and cannot be simply learned from a book. The religious teacher here is called the Lama.

Despite his obtaining all the information about opportunities to meditate Rahula's major interest was not advanced enough to discern what kind of spiritual classes he could attend. Although high on mushrooms during their conversation, his growing disenchantment with using drugs to get high had him guess that meditation in general might perhaps be a way to make the mind naturally clear and high; that interesting talk with Jim, while enjoying nature in the vicinity of Mount Anapurna, was the first and last time they ever saw each other, although it marked the beginning of a radical turning point in Rahula's life.

He was now eager to get back to Kathmandu immediately in order to sign up for the meditation course. Three days after meeting Jim, he was back there late that afternoon, and the next morning saw him taking a long walk out to the suburb Boudnath, which is named after the huge, ancient Buddhist Stupa[4], which is located just off the road in the middle of many shops. It dominates the skyline, one of the largest Stupa in the world, and has been a UNESCO World Heritage Site since 1979.

A large, at that time newly constructed, Tibetan Buddhist monastery rises among the rice paddies on a hill behind the Stupa, which Rahula found nearly deserted except for a handful of people doing work here and there. In the reception office, he met the person in charge of registering, a young shaven headed Canadian nun wearing the traditional burgundy colored robe of the Tibetan Monastic Order. She informed him of the rules to be

---

4   Stupa, Buddhist commemorative monument usually housing sacred relics associated with the Buddha or other saintly persons.

observed during the session: no use of drugs, no intimate contact with the opposite sex, a minimum of irrelevant conversation with other participants, and no leaving the hill premises for the town unless having the express permission of the course manager, which would, in any case be given only in an emergency. During the second half of the retreat, there would be a period of more intensive practice by observing the ten Buddhist precepts.

In Buddhism we find five precepts that are the basic training rules for all practicing lay people: they must refrain from destroying living creatures, from taking what is not given, from sexual misconduct, from incorrect speech, and from intoxicating drinks and drugs, which lead to carelessness.

The five further precepts are: refraining from eating after noon, from dancing, singing, making and listening to music, going to see entertainments, wearing garlands, using perfumes, and beautifying the body with cosmetics, lying in a high or luxurious sleeping place, and accepting gold and silver (money).

From the latter precepts, the only one relevant to Rahula was about eating, which meant no dinner. Moreover, they would only serve vegetarian food in the monastery. However, not eating meat or fish is not directly part of the precept. It was not even demanded by the historical Buddha and, thinking about the alms routes he must have taken, it is highly unlikely that he did not eat meat or fish. Among the different schools of the *Dhamma*, there are also different rules about the demands of vegetarianism. From the precept not to kill any living creature, the conclusion is drawn to refrain from eating meat or fish, but it is rather understood as refraining from them only if there has been (indirect) participation in the killing. It might sound a little strange to argued that if an animal were already dead and not slaughtered, then it is not quite the same thing as killing the animal oneself. However, one can say that, in *Theravada* Buddhism, vegetarianism is considered a personal choice.

For Rahula it was neither a problem not getting dinner nor eating only vegetarian food. He had already become a vegetarian since a trek he had been on before the Nepal meditation course near the Tibetan border. He told me the story:

"I was suffering from indigestion all the time, a lot of pain in my guts and a kind of diarrhea. Then one day, I stayed in a little guest house in a village that didn't really have a room and I had to sleep kind of in the kitchen. They had big chunks of goat meat hanging from the ceiling, kind of raw and ugly looking with blood dripping down from them. And then, that night, they made some rice with meat and vegetables and I saw the woman of the house with a big rusty knife and she was cutting off pieces of meat from above and throwing them into the cooking pot. And I said to myself: I am not eating that; I am not. And I only had rice that night and, from then on, no more meat."

But the greatest challenge he had to deal with of the five common precepts was the one prohibiting drug taking.

Now he would learn whether his strong six-year smoking habit was, which he sometimes wondered about, addictive or not. Up to that time, he had been sure he could quit any time he wanted to.

He had no real idea about the exact content of the course, what the participants would be learning and meditating upon and he tried not to speculate or create any fixed expectations about what it would or should be. In the afternoon, when he arrived at the venue where the course took place, he was assigned to sleep in a house at the bottom of a hill, a five-minute walk to the top. It was a building that, with only two large rooms, was totally empty except for a thick layer of straw covering the earthen floor and acting as a wall-to-wall mattress, all in all for twenty men. There was a single water tap nearby, which the villagers collected water from and washed under, and the participants were supposed to use it as well.

The formal opening began, after a light meal was served at 6:30 pm, with an introductory talk by the Lama, who would be the principal teacher. The name of the Lama, who has since become a recognized teacher or guru, is Lama Zopa Rinpoche. He was born in 1946 and was one of the monks that had to flee from Tibet due to the threat posed by the Chinese army after 1959. He is most notable as the co-founder and Spiritual Director of the Foundation for the Preservation of the *Mahayana* Tradition (FPMT) and oversees all of its activities.

In the tent, everyone was seated upon his or her own pillow, folded sleeping bag, blanket, etcetera, on top of the straw-covered floor. As is common practice, everyone was required, when the Lama entered, to rise quickly to their feet. Most of those in front (most of the newcomers sat in the back half) bent forward with their two palms touching as a gesture of respect. Being unfamiliar with this eastern protocol, Rahula, as most of those in the back, just watched as the teacher walked in and went to the front of the colorfully decorated altar. He stopped and faced the pantheon of Thankas behind the altar with the portrait of the Dalai Lama in the middle and prostrated himself on his hands and knees, touching his head to the ground three times. He then climbed up the ladder onto his slightly higher, quite large seat with a thick cushion and draped with fine cloth so that it looked more like a throne[5]. Once seated, the devoted ones up front, led by the monks and nuns, prostrated themselves fully flat on the floor three times in his direction.

For westerners, and Rahula would have been no exception, watching the prostrations must have made a strange kind of impression and seemed such a peculiar act: kneeling and then bowing in front of a Thanka or a Buddha statue made of clay or any other material, even gold. At least, in the beginning, it was for me. I once asked Bhante Rahula about it and he explained its significance to me very succinctly. It is, on one hand, a sign of respect for attaining the enlightenment of the historic Buddha and, on the other, for accepting his teaching and guidance. He said:

"And so you see it and you have that respect for the enlightened Buddha and for all the sacrifice he has made over many lifetimes—it inspires your faith, especially if it is a nice statue that has that essence of wisdom about it to remind you. Your bow is like aspiring to this kind of quality."

Then he added that on a deeper level it is also

---

5   Thanka is a piece of Tibetan art works, painted on cotton or silk fabrics using bright colors of many hues. It depicts various facts of Buddhism of mystic sect and is used as wall -decorations. For, Lamas Thanka is object of religious importance as an object of devotion, an aid to spiritual practice, and a bringer of blessings.

supposed to bring the additional benefit of a reduction in pride and arrogance, to humbly open oneself to the guidance of others and so become capable of learning and growing. The three acts of prostration stand for the 'Triple Gem' (*Buddha, Dhamma, Sangha*). After that explanation, I asked if I were supposed to do so as well and he answered: "It's up to you if you want to do it. If you don't, you don't have to."

Back to Rahula's first ever retreat in Nepal, he faced wakeup calls at 6 am, after which the participants were supposed to meditate by themselves and, after breakfast, read a book that the Lama gave out at the beginning of the course. Surprisingly, most of the content of the talks and the book material over the first few days concentrated on the basics of the Buddhist teaching that Rahula had studied in a general way when he wrote his paper on Buddhism back in college, although he had meanwhile more or less forgotten how the individual mind is involved in unlimited suffering, the source of which is the three mental poisons of ignorance, greed and hatred. He was further reminded of the doctrine of *Karma*, the natural law of cause and effect and how it operates in the body and mind within the context of the whole process of the *Samsara*.

In his meditations, he could easily see now how his past self-centered greed, lust and attachments had so often rebounded on him and those around him. He also contemplated world events of the past and present and saw how this law of *Karma*, especially its negative aspect, has reaped havoc on a global scale. By considering all these factors together, he began more easily to imagine how this strong mental force, powered by the ego's thirst and willpower to live, is involved in the *Samsara* cycle. He saw that the mind did not just originate out of nothing in this life nor will it just dissolve or become extinguished at death. For him, the theory of *Karma* and rebirth began to make more logical sense than the Christian theology of God's creation.

Perfect Human Rebirth was also a theme: how advanced it is to be born as a human being and that it depends on the *Karma* of morality, charity and friendliness that brought one into this life and now provides the opportunity for practicing more of the same and developing wisdom. That, however, depends on the favorable circumstances in one's life. Being born mentally retarded and deformed or handicapped in other ways or into such poverty or remote places where just staying alive takes all one's time and energy with little chance of learning about spiritual development or meditation is the contrary to this.

But to be born as a human being means having the potential to choose the path to attaining enlightenment. The Buddha himself made it totally clear: if there were no freedom of choice, the idea of a path of practice would make no sense. Rahula began to understand that people, in circumstances where the conditions are mostly favorable, waste this perfect opportunity through staying caught in the web of attachments, aversions, prejudice and ego-building they have woven themselves into.

In the second week of the course, the teaching and contemplation of one of the three stages of reality (*Anicca, Dukkha, Anatta*), the reality of impermanence and death, began in more detail. The teaching expounded that, when we die, we take nothing with us except our accumulated ignorance or wisdom. Furthermore, the time of our death is uncertain. The material body, made of the four elements, is so fragile and dependent on so many external factors as well as past *Karma* accumulated in the mind that we may die unexpectedly. There is a saying from an ancient Tibetan sage: "Tomorrow or the next life, who knows which will come first?"

Coming close to the awareness that the aspect of the present moment's impermanence in its relationship to confusion and suffering is even more relevant than relating it to the time of death and the next life, was sufficient for Rahula to know the direction he would now pursue. Thus, in his own words:

As I paid more attention to this, I began to relate in a still deeper way to the Buddha's profound Dhamma.

To accompany this teaching, we were given a particular type of death meditation to practice. We imagined ourselves undergoing the process of conscious death from the last hour to being reborn according to our last thought or strongest habits. This included visualizing the deluded negative mind being spontaneously reborn into the lower realms as an animal, a hungry ghost and in the various classifications of hell. We had read the vivid descriptions of the deprivation and tortuous suffering experienced by the creatures in those realms. And in meditation, when we came to that point, we were to try and visualize it with as much color and detail as possible, going through each, one at a time. We were to try and create or arouse a simulated feeling for what the suffering would really be like. The purpose for this was to activate in the mind a sense of seriousness about how we die, to motivate us to keep our minds purged of the kind of negative thoughts which would generate our rebirth there.

My initial reaction to doing this meditation was somewhat skeptical. I recalled articles from western psychologists who talked about the dangers of this mental manipulation. They said it could trigger off psychic shock and other unpredictable mental and physical disorders in certain types of people. I did not necessarily believe in all the vivid descriptions or even that there were such miserable hells existing somewhere in time and space, some of which were really outlandish. I figured that, whether real or not, these contemplations were a skillful ploy for goading people to wake up from their folly. I had already experienced much usefulness in the previous meditation exercises we had been doing and because of this, I was beginning to more or less surrender any resistance of my western conditioning to the Lama. I had faith that he knew from some kind of personal experience what he was talking about and, therefore, tried to do the meditation as thoroughly and with as much vivid detail as I could muster up.

In a few people, this kind of subconscious probing did indeed trigger off spectacular physical and mental reactions. During one of the group meditation periods on this subject I heard someone begin to cry, which turned into uncontrolled sobbing lasting for sometime. I found out afterwards via the gossip grapevine that a girl had been doing the crying.

The meditation had indeed gone deep and touched a very sensitive nerve or perhaps past life memory, triggering off the uncontrollable crying. One English guy really freaked out: he left the hill and went into Kathmandu. Rumor had it that this guy, wearing only his underwear, went into a restaurant on freak street, stood up on a table and pissed all over the floor. It seems he was subdued by a couple of good Samaritan Christians before the police came and was escorted to the seclusion of a 'home for

lost souls' which the Born Again Christians had set up there in Kathmandu.

What this illustrated is that we all have so much accumulated suffering and trauma from the past locked up inside the subconscious mind which must be released or purified before we can attain real mental freedom, the end of all suffering.

During these first two weeks everything that I had

been hearing, reading about and meditating upon gradually began to take some kind of shape and started to have an increasing affect on me. In the beginning, all these Buddhist ideas remained in my head as 'out-there' philosophy. Now, it seemed to be shifting from the brain down into the heart as a wordless feeling; it was starting to move inside, upsetting the applecart of the routine mind. Each Dhamma talk, each new theme of contemplation, each period of meditation was like another piece of a jigsaw puzzle being fitted into place or like a pimple coming to a head. It was as though something deep down inside was beginning to loosen itself from the obscure murky depths and rise to the surface. It was a vague feeling and I could not get a hold of it or put it into words, being very subtle and evasive. It was similar to the experience of having the answer to a question on the tip of the tongue, but not being able to recall it enough to express it.

On Thanksgiving night, this crescendo came to a climax. I was sitting there as usual, listening to the Lama speaking about the deepest meaning of religion and was very absorbed in what he was saying, feeling quite relaxed and buoyant. All of a sudden, after a particular sentence, it was like the last piece of that jigsaw puzzle was fit into place, like that ripe pimple bursting. After an initial few moments of something like mental shock, I exclaimed to myself, "Wow, wow, wow, I've been ignorant all of my life!" The whole esoteric meaning of religion or purpose of life seemed to become clear, to reveal itself. It appeared to be the unmistakable answer to all I had unconsciously wanted to know. I sat there no longer even paying attention to the Lama's discourse. All I could think about was how stupid, ignorant and spiritually blind I had been all of my life, deludedly following my ego's desires and caught in the web of conditionality. After the Lama had finished his talk and everyone went out for the break, all I could do was lie down and continue to feel the liberating effects of that experience. It felt like a fivehundredpound block of cement which I had been carrying on my shoulders for a long time had just been pushed off. I wrote down in my blue notebook: 'this is Thanksgiving Day, the first day of the rest of my life. Today I am reborn'.

Chapter 6

"Out of this moment, when the world melted away all around him, when he stood alone like a star in the sky, out of this moment of cold and despair ... he felt this had been the last tremor of the awakening, the last struggle of this birth. And it was not long until he walked again in long strides, started to proceed swiftly and impatiently, heading no longer for home, no longer to his father, no longer back."

This scenario of rebirth that happens to the protagonist of the famous novel *Siddhartha* by Hermann Hesse might be comparable to Rahula's. What occurred in both looks like fate, but it is not, although Westerners commonly tend to confuse the term fate and its meaning with what it really is: *Karma*, as it is understood in Buddhist teaching.

It was also *Karma* that brought me, 25 years later, to attend a *Vipassana* meditation retreat with a monk from the USA who was reborn in Nepal following his experience with his first *Vipassana* retreat. Unlike him, I did not feel my rebirth, but I felt something during the course and I said these words to myself repeatedly when I wanted again and again to give up. I said: 'then you will be dead'.

When I later talked to Rahula about how hard the first couple of meditation retreats were for me, I praised him for being so brave as to go on a retreat for a whole month and then asked if he had had any second thoughts, he replied:

"One month! I wasn't even thinking about that. I mean, if you ask people to go on a two-day retreat, they worry a lot and say 'Oh, can I manage that?'. I didn't see it like that. It was only the desire to meditate and think about what kind of meditation it would be."

"But how was it with the drug-taking?" I asked.

"Yes, that was the main thing because you could not come to the meditation course with drugs. That was the challenge. But I wanted that. I said 'okay, it has to be like that.'"

"So, it wasn't a sacrifice for you at that moment—giving up drugs?"

"No, it was something I wanted to do."

"And didn't you have a hard time—sometimes thinking 'oh no, couldn't I just have one little joint'?"

"No, just after the course. Because during the course I had some."

"You had some?"

"Yes, I mean I had some that I carried to the

course. But I had it deep down at the bottom of my pack. Just as a kind of … I don't know what …"

"Emergency."

"Yes, emergency. But I had forgotten about it because I got so interested in the daily meditations and readings and my mind was busy with the *Dhamma*. That's when I realized I didn't have to get high on drugs because the *Dhamma* always got me high. That helped me to understand why people took drugs, because the mind is not naturally high. It is full of problems and they take drugs or drink or whatever in order to get out of it temporally. But when you meditate and do Yoga, when you practice *Sila*, your mind gets into this higher vibration that means freedom from all those thoughts."

"But you said later …"

"Yes, after the course. Then I took a hit. In Katmandu. I didn't want to start again, but I wondered what it might be like to smoke something after a month of not taking anything. I went into one of those hippie cafés, careful not to let anybody from the meditation course see me, and I rolled a joint and smoked it. But I wasn't happy with it. It kind of made me back off a little and it didn't really do much. That's what I realized. Although once or twice, like in Goa, I did it again I had that … it brought me down actually. So I was ready to stop. But this experience helped me to reinforce the idea that the *Dhamma* can be a replacement for getting high. But it's a different type of high, of course. The feeling in meditation goes much deeper. It is also good for the body too. Your behavior becomes more attuned to the *Dhamma*."

"You mean it could be called the 'Buddha nature'? Not Buddha Gautama, but the Buddha nature?"

"Right, right, yeah, because the *Dhamma* ultimately is that."

The *Karma* that led Rahula to the retreat was the action of what was caused within him. The Sanskrit word *Karma* means 'action'. Things we choose to do, say or think set *Karma* in motion. The law of *Karma* is therefore a law of cause and effect. The term *fate* is in fact just the effect, the result. When Rahula and I talked about the impact that it had on him when he became acquainted with the *Dhamma*, he described it in the following way:

"The drug taking, you know, had clouded my common sense. I might easily have been killed by an overdose or put in prison, and so on. I got to change my mind, I got to get off drugs and all these things came together at the same time, you know. Then I was on my way to India and I think that's why I was attracted to going to Nepal: I heard about this meditation course and, within two weeks, was listening to the lectures and thinking about it, and that was—boom—something clicked in my mind."

The American Buddhist monk, Thanissaro Bhikkhu born in 1949, well known for his translations of almost one thousand *Suttas*, has described *Karma*[6] in this way: *The early Buddhist notion of Karma focused on the liberating potential of what the mind is doing with every moment. Who you are—what you come from—is not anywhere near as important as the mind's motives for what it is doing right now. Even though the past may account for many of the inequalities we see in life, our measure as human beings is not the hand we've been dealt, for that hand can change at any moment. We take our own measure by how well we play the hand we've got. If you're suffering, you try not to continue the unskillful mental habits that would keep that particular karmic feed-back going.*

In 1973 in Nepal, Scott DuPrez, still an American hippie, took his own measure not only to become a monk, but also to become a re-markable and in a way innovative teacher concerning the way to use Yoga exercises for the mindfulness of the body's sensations.

The retreat I attended with the then Bhante Rahula was announced to contain meditation and Yoga. The latter I had no idea about and expressed my concerns to a long-term Rahula

---

6   "Karma", by Thanissaro Bhikkhu. Access to Insight (BCBS Edition), 8 March 2011

student before the beginning of the Noble Silence, with which we all had to comply, but she said that "it wouldn't be that bad."

She was right and I, by the way, have been practicing Yoga ever since. When I first saw Rahula, he looked exactly what I imaged a practitioner of Yoga, a Yogi, looks like: tall, bald, and skinny.

The Venerable Bhante Gunnaratana, abbot of the Bhavana forest monastery in West Virginia, known by everybody as Bhante G., used to put it like this: "lean with veins showing all over his body".

While I was observing his calm, forthright and courteous behavior for the first time, I came to sense from the first moment that he really was the reliable teacher he was praised up to be, but he was not there mainly as a Yogi, but as a *Vipassana* teacher. *Vipassana* is one of India's most ancient techniques of insight meditation. Its practice, which uses the mindfulness of breathing, thoughts, feelings and actions, was rediscovered by the historical Buddha in order to gain insight into the true nature of reality, which, in his teaching, as already mentioned, is impermanence, suffering, and the realization of the non-self.

Later, when we were once walking together and talking about it, he elaborated on this kind of meditation:

"Insight meditation is about observing how

your mind creates its perception of the world. The outside world is a projection of our mental processes. It comes from insight. So normally we see all these things as having an external existence, but insight meditation allows us to observe how our mental processes start from within the self and its projection, which we see as the external world, is really the projection of the internal view."

Then he explained that first you have to attain insight because the mind operates according to the body's nervous system. When you are grounded and concentrated in the body in the present moment, then you can more clearly see how the mind recognizes phenomena such as getting caught up in likes and dislikes, and you can observe this with some detachment so that you don't react so quickly to things.

Because of my experience of his guidance during meditation, I then asked whether it was important to sit in a certain position, especially upright with the spine. Rahula cut in on me with:

"To keep the nervous system relaxed in its optimal working condition in order to prevent bending or slouching, so that the mind's consciousness slows down and gets clearer. Sitting straight and alert keeps the mind and the nervous system clear and in a relaxed position so that you can observe clearly without distortions and distractions. *Vipassana* or insight

119

meditation is the same, but the word *Vipassana* means seeing things as they really are. That means observing our mind creating our pictures or reactions to the world. Bodily access is the anchor to hold our attention to the present moment. The body and breathing occur in the present moment, so we use them as an anchor. Only our mind gets distracted easily, but if it is grounded by and connected with the breathing body, then it is like sitting in a movie theater and watching the screen: watching the activities of your body and mind in a more objective and distant way; observing an itch or a pain without reacting to it; seeing how the bodily sensations change and how the mind is thinking about them. As the observer, you will find this space, a mental space without reacting. That is the main thing: observation without reaction and clearly seeing the cause and effect, the 'domino effects' that happen to our body and mind."

"So," I interrupted, " observing the change to bodily sensations is the main thing."

"Yes, the likes and dislikes and thinking to bring in the past and/or future connected to any particular sensation. In meditation, you observe all that without adding to the process."

"Like with noises that we hear," I said, "whether they are the pleasant chirpings of birds or unpleasant traffic sounds. In a state of meditation, we can perceive them for what they really are: not likeable or dislikeable, but just noises, right?"

"Yeah, you train your mind to recognize the noise. But of course you can also see the mind labeling the object. If you hear something: 'Oh that is a car driving by, that's a dog barking', those are perceptions. Normally, because of the perception, you start thinking about the object. Maybe fear comes into your mind—or desire. But, with this training, we are able to observe those things for what they are and not get caught up in them."

"The deal in meditation as I understand it is observing briefly what happens and then immediately going back to the breathing ..."

"Yes, staying connected to the body is how we can transform our common actions, how we react to everything, how to learn just by watching, observing, reacting and transferring the nervous system to a more mellow and relaxed level of awareness. There is more natural perception as a natural state of our nervous system and consciousness. So that is the more natural mind than the educated. This state of our mind, if it is not disturbed, is natural."

When Rahula came into contact with *Vipassana* in the East and continued to study Yoga, he was made aware that practicing both together would not only be unpopular but also unwelcome. Nevertheless, after he started to practice meditation on a regular basis, he added Yoga exercises because for him it was a reasonable match. On his second meditation retreat, Yoga exercises were in fact not allowed. It was the *Vipassana* retreat conducted by S. N. Goenka, the teacher that Jim had been talking about in Tatopani. Rahula already knew about the Yoga ban from him but could not really understand why doing little exercises would hurt. According to Goenka, however, it would create unnecessary extra distraction. Rahula said it was interesting to see in his mind the initial resistance thrown up to this request which contradicted his opinion, but he reluctantly took Goenka's word for it. Later, after the course was over, Goenka told him that it was okay to do Yoga exercises on his own, as long as he did not get too preoccupied with the body and let it take time away from the meditation sittings.

Rahula went to this retreat in 1974 when Goenka (1924 to 2013) had just started teaching *Vipassana* meditation three years before. He would later become one of the most influential teachers of *Vipassana* meditation. In 1976, he opened his first meditation center, *Dhamma* Giri, in India. Nowadays there are more than one hundred permanent *Vipassana* meditation centers in countries all over the world, such as the USA, Canada, France, Germany, Spain, Italy, Switzerland, Sweden and the United Kingdom, to name but a few, which teach it in the tradition of Goenka.

The belief that Yoga could preoccupy the body and as such distract too much from *Vipassana* meditation did not accord with Rahula's opinions and experience. In the face of this belief, he intensified his practice with a book he found in a bookstore in Bombay (Mumbai). The title was *Yoga Self Taught*, written by the Indian Yoga teacher Sri Yogendra. It seemed to Rahula to be well written and contained many neat pictorial illustrations of the various postures and exercises. It also described a system of rhythmic breathing which coordinated in- and exhalation with the movements involved. It looked and sounded interesting because it seemed to add a new dimension to his practice that he was not aware of before.

The book was attractive because of another feature: a short but clear explanation of the philosophy behind Yoga—being a complete practice that purifies and integrates both aspects of the body and mind to achieve Self-Realization and *Moksha*[7]. What harm could come from practicing Yoga anyway?

Why was Yoga not welcome as a joint discipline with *Vipassana*? The answer is not easy

---

7   The term in Hinduism referring to various forms of emancipation, liberation, release, and to freedom from *Samsara*, the cycle of death and rebirth.

because nowadays, at least in the West, *Vipassana* and Yoga are considered a good combination. It is not least to Bhante Rahula's merit that this common combination is enjoyed today and it would not presumably have come about without his profound training in the field of Yoga.

The big break that put Yoga into his future *Vipassana* meditation practice came in Colombo, in the building that Rahula visited to report for the registration of non-Commonwealth visitors to Sri Lanka, when he picked up a tourist pamphlet describing what was happening in Colombo that month. While leafing through the events calendar, he noticed a one-month Yoga course which was being conducted by Dr. Swami Gitananda from Pondicherry, South India. Rahula described his impression at this moment:

"The same reaction came over me as when I had first heard of the Tibetan meditation course; my eyes instantly lit up; it sounded like just the opportunity I'd been waiting for—to study Yoga under a qualified teacher. It seemed to be presenting itself on a silver platter."

It was also worth his while that the course was being taught by a real Indian Yoga Master. Unfortunately it had already begun the day before, but he hoped he could still be admitted. He dropped by the address the first thing the next day to inquire. At the Yoga ashram, an American woman named Meenakshi, who happened to be the Swami's wife, replied:

"The course is already full and the Swamiji doesn't like admitting latecomers".

But she asked Rahula to wait anyway while she went to inform the Swami. When she returned several minutes later, she told him he could talk with the Swamiji straight away and personally present his case. Rahula felt a little nervous meeting him face to face and tried to imagine the proper etiquette for presenting himself in front of an Indian Guru. He described the situation like this:

"I did not have any flowers or fruit to offer, which I knew was the accepted tradition, and I wasn't sure if the standard Buddhist-style prostrations would be appropriate. I decided to greet him with the respectful Namaste and bow. Upon knocking on the closed door of the back room, a deep voice called out, 'Come in'. Once inside, I greeted the Swami with the Namaste; and he returned it with a big, friendly smile and said: 'Hi, please be seated', while pointing to a mat on the floor. The Swami was quite imposing, seated in a chair looking almost like my projected image of an Indian Yogi—shoulder-length, white, flowing hair with a matching bushy beard and wearing the orange cloth of a Sanyassin. Though I believe Meenakshi had already recounted the situation to him, I repeated my desire to join the course. He explained frankly how it was not

125

ordinarily his policy to admit latecomers for fear of upsetting the 'status quo' and that he had already given some important instruction anyway. But if I were sincere about staying for the rest of the entire course and attended all the classes punctually, starting with the next class in just a few minutes, then he would consent. I agreed of course. He inquired further whether I had any previous Yoga experience. I mentioned the little bit I had picked up from the book. He did not seem much impressed and commented that proper Yoga necessitated personal imparting and guidance from a qualified teacher—and that those were few and far between these days."

The Swami was, as Rahula said, a perfectionist, a stickler for details, described each new technique and practice very thoroughly and expected the students to listen carefully and perform it exactly the way he had taught. He emphasized that Yoga was an exact science and entailed a conscious evolution of the self. He criticized western Yoga fans who cut corners and modified Yoga to suit themselves, saying: "We need a western Yoga." He dubbed slip-shod or haphazard practice as 'Bhoga Yoga' or 'Armchair Yoga'!

Rahula learned a lot of yogic cleansing techniques, including a salt-water purge of the entire gastro-intestinal tract. This was a kind of 'spring cleaning' for the body and was normally followed by a period of fasting; he also learned cleansing techniques for the nose and sinus passages.

He heard how all the practices in the science of Yoga are based upon the universal reality of *Prana*, the invisible, all-pervasive life force which sustains all forms of life—human, animal, plant and even mineral. He referred to it as 'cosmic plasma' or a kind of rarified electrical energy that binds all of the elements of creation together and gives them life. We receive most of the *Prana* the body needs through breathing, but small amounts are taken in and absorbed from the food we eat, especially raw food, and the water we drink.

Prana circulates through the body via an extensive network of invisible etheric channels called *Nadis*. Under normal circumstances, *Prana* that flows in the *Nadis* set patterns to perform various vital functions, but, unlike the circulation of the blood, it can be rerouted and directed by the mind. A high concentration of *Prana* in a particular painful or diseased area can be an effective healing power. *Pranayama* (the concept implying a set of breathing techniques where the breath is intentionally altered in order to produce specific results) is then the conscious, controlled movement of *Prana* in various prescribed patterns and rhythms to insure the optimum health and well being of the entire body/mind organism. *Pranayama* is not merely deep breathing exercises; although it enters with the air, it includes visualization or awareness of the energy as it is directed through the *Nadis*.

Rahula wrote in his autobiography that all of this was fascinating for him. However, let me add, it was not just that. It was key information, proven by his own experiences in his practice and therefore exerted great influence on his future teaching. All his students know 'three-part lobular breathing' or, as he named it, three-part breathing. According to Dr. Swami Gitananda, the 'sine qua non' of Yoga is based upon mastering three-part lobular breathing. This means breathing into the three major lobes of the lungs, the lower, middle and higher, in a rhythmic fashion. Each of the three lung sections governs *Prana* and blood circulation to a corresponding area of the body. If we fail to breathe in one or more of the lobes, then the respective body parts will not get the required amount of blood, oxygen and *Prana* to maintain themselves properly.

Rahula went over this lobular breathing many times during the course and was taught different postures designed to help stimulate or force the air to go into the three lung sections. His comment was:

"Hell, I had never even known what real deep breathing was nor that I had these different lung lobes, etcetera. For all intents and purposes, the lungs were just an elastic bag that we breathed in and out of. This was a new revelation for me, and I could feel the difference

128

once I practiced a little and got the hang of it."

This revelation leads to the, for his students, famous term 'three-part breathing'. Countless numbers of Rahula's students not only breathe that way during the Yoga classes in the retreats he conducts, but also in meditation sessions. Rahula's students certainly know this kind of breathing, but they also probably experience the effect of the energy that it brings—an effect you can become aware of during a meditation session. Meditation, especially, takes a considerable amount of time, even two hours and more for the advanced students. It is therefore consistent, because of that energy, to start every session with that method of breathing after seating yourself in the right position. It is helpful to do this breathing again between periods of meditation. You might from time to time get tired, catch yourself bending or slouching from the upright position, or becoming aware of extended mental distraction; this is when the three-part breathing discipline can recoup the energy you have obviously lost.

There is more. Rahula not only recommends his students this kind of breathing for the time of the retreat courses but also for their daily life because it is the easiest and most effective thing to practice. Not just the physical in- and exhaling of oxygen, but from time to time the setting of a life-sustaining energy in motion for a positive performance that can be achieved at any time.

Bearing this in mind and also knowing the important role focused breathing performs in the practice of Buddhist meditation, there is no reason at all why Yoga should disturb the practice of *Vipassana* meditation.

Maybe the aversion of Buddhist monks and teachers to Yoga has to do with the Yoga concept originating in Hindu history. Rahula was convinced by what he learned from the Swami about the six or eight various branches of the holistic science of Yoga and said:

"The way it seemed to confidently and expertly expound and integrate the various aspects of body and mind purification/training made it appear to be truly the granddaddy of all sciences."

He saw more clearly, on a deeper level, the fundamental relationship between the body and the mind; they are like two sides of a coin and it is necessary to treat them so in the process of spiritual growth and eventual Enlightenment. But there are similarities and differences in how Yoga and Buddhism approach and treat the matter of Spiritual Awakening and liberation from *Samsara*.

Buddhism does not concern itself with purifying the body first or directly as in Yoga. It appears to be chiefly concerned with eradicating the unwholesome elements in the mind firstly and directly by meditation to achieve the end of suffering and the ultimate happiness of *Nirvana*. In Buddhism there is neither space nor need to mention anything about a God or a Supreme Self or Soul (Atman).

Yoga, on the other hand, does have as a principal concept the existence an Inner Self or Atman (our true nature as consciousness, authentic self or soul) and often uses the various words as synonyms for God (Brahma, Vishnu, Shiva, etcetera) as the creator, preserver and destroyer of the universe. Self-realization on the yogic path requires complete faith in the Atman and surrender to God.

So in general there is a contradiction in terms between the Non-self or Emptiness doctrines of Buddhism and the Self-Realization of Yoga (and Hinduism). On the other hand, they both claim emancipation from the flesh and the attainment of everlasting peace and happiness.

Having this in mind, Rahula wrote in his autobiography:

I wondered if there was really any fundamental difference. How could there be two separate Truths or Ultimate Realities? ... I felt in either case the ultimate goal for me was still a long way off. Whether there was a crucial, irreconcilable difference or not would all eventually come out in the wash, as the saying goes, as it became clearer in my continued studies, practice and personal experience of each. For the time being, I was content with practicing Yoga to purify and strengthen the body/nervous system and the Buddhist meditation to eliminate mental defilements, decrease attachments and cultivate Wisdom.

In the years following more training in the *Dhamma* via intense meditation practice until teaching it himself, there was never a situation that caused him to abandon his first impression that both of them, Yoga and Buddhist meditation, can easily and helpfully be practiced together.

As far as I am concerned, Yoga is a generated extension in Buddhist meditation practice because, in order to clarify the mind, the body is needed as an anchor, as Rahula teaches. Even though it is not a necessary condition for Enlightenment, why should one neglect this profound device to attain liberation?

Rahula was, as we can see, very impressed by the course he took in Colombo. However, he was not entirely content because it was too short. The teacher himself said that this was primarily intended to be a whirlwind introduction to the variety, scope and practical application of the various aspects of Yoga. All the material presented in this one-month course had been condensed from a standard, full six-month teacher-training course that he taught in a slower, more detailed manner. This course at his ashram in Pondicherry begins on October 1st of each year. He added that six months were usually sufficient to get a good foundation in these teachings and become competent enough to instruct others if one so desired and made a sincere effort. He even offered a Yoga teacher certificate to those who successfully completed the six months of training.

Rahula was so convinced of the concept of Yoga regarding its positive influence on the body and mind that there was no question of him not taking this opportunity. So he went to Swami Gitananda's ashram in Pondicherry in 1974 and 1975.

From his rebirth in Nepal on Thanksgiving Day, 1973, he first went to Bodh Gaya to take the opportunity to see the Dalai Lama, who, as Rahula had heard, was expected there. Bodh Gaya is a special place, tempting to visit anyway, because it is the holiest place for Buddhists. It is famous since it is the place where Gautama Buddha is said to have obtained Enlightenment under a fig tree that became known as the Bodhi (Enlightenment) tree. Apart from this Buddhist significance, the town is also well-known for the famous Hindu Vishnupad Mandir temple.

From Bodh Gaya, Rahula went to the Goenka course in Pratapgarh and after that revived his old idea to spend time there in Goa. The plan in the past had derived, of course, from the fact that Goa was famous for its hippie lifestyle that could be led on the marvelous beaches at that time. Although he was no

133

longer a hippie, the idea of Goa was still appealing as a suitable place to live simply in a thatched hut, in pleasant weather, going naked on the beach, where he could continue meditation and get back to more Yoga exercises, which he had sorely missed during the Goenka course.

He was wondering a little if he might be able to proceed properly or fall for the sensuality that the island would certainly offer plus the overabundance of drugs. He knew these things were readily available there and could be a strong temptation, but he put aside his doubts about whether he could resist all the sensual lures and considered that the outcome would be able to demonstrate the strength of his practice.

He traveled by train down to Bombay and from there by ship to Panjim, the capital of Goa. Apart from the old plan to head to Goa, there was also a further factor influencing his heading south that would make the stopover in Goa a reasonable decision. He had heard that there were a couple of *Vipassana* meditation centers in Sri Lanka where conditions were favorable for intensive practice. One of the centers was reported to have a good teacher who spoke English. It was also supposed to be relatively easy to obtain a visa for six months, especially if one intended to study Buddhism. The Ceylonese or Sinhalese people were predominantly Buddhist and the government was supportive of foreigners in this respect. While his Indian visa would expire at the end of March anyway, it seemed to be the most viable alternative, a natural next step.

The goal, the only goal, namely to practice more meditation used to be the reason for going to Sri Lanka. And so he went there. After he was attracted in Colombo by the offer to study Yoga and partake in the one-month course, he followed his original plan, the only exception to it being that he went back to India for the six months of Yoga instruction in Pondicherry.

By the end of that intensive course, Rahula had developed a habit of seeing how everything that happened to him and the world fit into the Buddhist and Yoga world view. He said:

"I had read the English newspaper once in a while and heard bits and pieces of current world events as Swamiji, who read the paper every day, would comment on them from time to time and these *Dhamma* truths sunk deeper in. I thought indeed the majority of the human race is mad, blindly driven by the fires of ego-ignorance, greed, jealousy, and hatred. I pondered over my own past—how I had gotten here and speculating where it might all lead."

At the end of March, Swami Gitananda initiated the group into the advanced *Laya*

Yoga Kriyas, which Rahula described as follows:

"These practices are designed to raise the *Kundalini*[8] spiritual force up the hollow center of the spinal column (*Sushumna Nadi*) to pass through the seven *Chakras* to the Thousand Petalled Lotus at the crown of the head. When Cosmic Awareness becomes fully established at this crown (*Chakra*), this is the Yogi's Enlightenment and liberation from *Samsara*, termed Brahma *Nirvana*. These Laya Yoga Kriyas were supposed to be the highest and consummate tantric practices for achieving this. All the other things we were doing such as the *Pranayamas*, *Chakra* awareness etcetera were only to purify the *Chakra* or nervous system, to prepare the groundwork for the 'final blow'. The experience of 'awaking the *Kundalini*' has been described in some popular books as being like a lightning bolt shooting up the spine, or at least a slower, hot, and sometimes painful ascendance. These *Kriyas* required a great deal of concentration and breath (*Prana*) control. Although I practiced them continuously for a few weeks, I never had any such radical experience. However, after thirty minutes or an hour of powerful concentration, I was left in a very effortless and blissful meditative state and

8   *Kundalini,* the yogic life force that is held to lie coiled at the base of the spine until it is aroused and sent to the head to trigger enlightenment

out-of-the-body feeling, which I could reach all the same by an hour of strong *Vipassana* awareness."

In the subsequent meditation Rahula did in Sri Lanka, before the interval with the Yoga course, he found a deep awareness of what he was supposed to be and where to go in the future. About his experience with the Yoga instruction he said: "I had always considered Buddhist meditation as my path for developing wisdom and attaining Enlightenment while Yoga was primarily a complementary support, purifying the 'body temple'. Compared to *Vipassana*, all these *Pranayama* breathing routines, concentration and meditation techniques, *Kriyas*, talk about *Chakras* and raising the *Kundalini* seemed too complicated and perhaps unnecessary. I went along with it all and tried my level best to get all possible experience and benefit from them—I was open to anything. I knew there must be something to it as it was such a highly evolved, technical, exact system; I didn't think it had only an imagined result. But it obviously wasn't the only path and maybe not mine, at least in all its aspects and fine details."

Chapter 7

„You can do what you want, but you can't want what you want" is my poetic summary of the ideas presented by the German philosopher Arthur Schopenhauer in his work *The World as Will and Representation*. He was one of the first thinkers in the West to be influenced by Indian philosophies, essentially and especially Buddhism. His ideas were on the same track when it comes to the cornerstone of Buddhist teaching, the dependent origination: "Nothing exists for itself and independently, nothing is single and detached".

The term *will* in the title of his standard work should not be confused with *want* or *free will*. It is just a term he had chosen for the movement of the world, of the *Samsara* or the karmic entanglement. Whatever arises, arises dependent on conditions; everything that exists, exists in dependence on the conditional. In "*World as Will*", 'will' means the key to all existence. From this principle, the *will* is the inner nature of the body as an appearance in time and space. So the inner reality of all material appearances is *will* and means the 'will to live'.

Rahula wanted to go to Sri Lanka and promptly did so. This was already preordained by the potential inherent in karmic determination. After arriving in Sri Lanka by ferry from India, Rahula first went to the ancient capital of Lanka, Anuradhapura to visit the large sacred park area called Maha Megha Vana, where an ancient Bodhi tree is located. It is, as the legend goes, in fact a seedling of the original in Bodh Gaya that was brought to Lanka in the 2nd century B.C. by the daughter of King Ashoka, Sanghamitra. Ashoka used to be a warrior and he conquered kingdom after kingdom. After becoming aware of all the violence he had inflicted upon thousands and thousands of people, he learned about the Buddhist teaching. He ceased fighting and, instead, spread the *Dhamma* all over India and surrounding regions such as Sri Lanka, to where he sent one of his sons and this daughter that brought the seedling.

Anyway, the tree (Jaya Sri Maha Bodhi) stands for the original Tree of the Enlightenment, which was the ancient Bodhi Tree of India in Bodh Gaya, where Buddha Shakyamuni attained enlightenment. It was destroyed by Thishyarakkha, a widow of King Ashoka, jealous of the time the Emperor spent there, according to one tradition. However, there are other legends as well, but it is agreed that the original tree was destroyed and a new planted in its place. The tree that grows at Bodh Gaya today was planted in 1881 by a British archaeologist using a shoot from the Sri Lanka tree after the previous one had died of old age a few years before.

Another inspiring landmark in the park, near the Bodhi tree, is the huge Ruvanveliseya Stupa that stands over one hundred and fifty feet high and is surrounded by an impressive stone wall of elephants standing side by side around a huge square compound. Rahula visited this large park area in the off-tourist season at the end of March and found it basically deserted.

At the same time of year, but ages later, I had the pleasure of being in this beautiful holy temple complex myself. I was lucky enough to experience it on the night of a full moon. In the Buddhist tradition, the most significant events occur at full moon: Buddha's birth, enlightenment and death occur on the full moon days of the month Vesak, which corresponds to the month of May. Every day of the full moon in Sri Lanka is an official holiday and on each of these days the Buddhist people visit one of its many temples. The full moon in May, the Vesak Festival, is the most sacred Buddhist festival of all.

I came to the Bodhi tree temple at dusk. The tree itself, next to the temple, is supported by iron poles and is impressive in appearance. The air in the temple was filled with the scent of hundreds of candles and incense sticks as well as countless people all dressed in white, paying reverence to the Buddha by bestowing flowers at the feet of the statues. In spite of the huge number of people in the temple, I had never experienced such a peaceful atmosphere. Being in the midst of the crowd, I felt a special meditative aura. Wandering around the area, I felt it more intensely, which invited me to stay much longer than intended, sitting on this full moon night at the feet of the big Stupa in Anuradhapura.

When Rahula arrived in Sri Lanka, he had the address and recommendation for the *Vipassana* Meditation Centre in Kanduboda, which situated in the countryside about sixteen miles from Colombo. The Center was started around 1956 when some Burmese monks came to Sri Lanka to teach meditation. These Bhikkhus were disciples of the Venerable Mahasi Sayadaw, the author of *Practical Insight Meditation*, a reputed Arahat and originator of this particular technique using the rise and fall of the abdomen. They came upon invitation to reintroduce the practice of meditation, which had all but died out due to the heavy Christian missionary activity of the last several hundred years.

That center was recommended and chosen because there was an English-speaking monk working there. Rahula wanted to stay there for a training course without knowing how long it would or could last. Anyway, he first postponed his appearance due to the two-month-long Yoga course I mentioned in the last chapter. When finally arriving at the center, he was made very welcome by the Venerable Sivali, who Rahula described as an "English speaking, middle-aged but youngish looking monk".

Rahula learned it would be possible to stay for a period of three weeks. Kanduboda was one of only two regular meditation centers for Westerners and the most popular, hence the imposition of the time limit. Sivali expected the students to observe the ten precepts, which Rahula knew from Kopan in Nepal, plus no talking with the other student meditators, writing letters or reading books. Practicing Yoga was not allowed either. All these prohibitions were intended to cultivate an uninterrupted mindfulness. Kanduboda was also a monastery with a number of monks. Hence, the students had to follow the rule for monks that stipulated not eating any solid food after the noon meal, just a cup of black tea would be served in the afternoon and evening.

Rahula had earlier been greatly intrigued when, in the village of Tatopani in Nepal, he heard about the technique of *Vipassana* meditation from Jim. In Bodh Gaya he kept his ears open to all the narratives from other Westerners about their experience with Buddhist meditations and it was then that the Goenka course came into focus for him.

These talks excited his interest in *Vipassana* even more, because this specific method of mental training seemed to be a direct, less mystical and ritualistic approach to developing wisdom than the Tibetan practices. There was no mention of various Buddha and Bodhisattvas, no need for saving all sentient beings, repeating mantras or creating complex visualizations, although it was exactly that kind of meditation the Lamas in Kopan had warned Rahula about as being inferior. They called it the approach to one's own selfish liberation. Anyway, he felt it right, and when I asked him later about the main difference, he said:

"*Vipassana* was more intellectual; all these theories, learning all the different things and thinking about life and all that. It is more about getting into contact with the subtle vibration and developing more kinds of awareness. That was the difference; you may look at it like this: the Tibetan course is like hooking a fish, you know. The fish bites the hook. But then, if it is a big fish you have to struggle and reel it in. The Tibetan course I think is like that. Their hooking me on the *Dhamma* and the *Theravada* practices was like slowly reeling in the fish."

"What do you think is the difference between *Theravada* and *Mahayana*?"

"It depends on the person. For me, the *Maha-yana* teaching has implicit compassion and suffering and rebirth and its disciples dedicate their lives to the *Dhamma*. It is like laying a good foundation, which for some people is enough, and some people whereas others go ahead and continue this and try a kind of tantric practice, because it is a kind of meditation that involves visualization, chanting mantras, doing Pujas[9], making Guru devotion, and dedicating one's life to others in terms of the *Bodhicitta* (enlightenment-mind). *Theravada* is more about working on yourself and using your own energy, and it's also more kind of like astir, kind of like ascetic you know. It is a stricter discipline."

Rahula first approached *Vipassana* meditation in its original practice, based on *Satipatthana Sutta*, in Kanduboda. The Goenka course, however, offers the one and only practice taught in meditation centers worldwide: the body scan method. This technique starts by placing attention at the crown of the head for a few minutes to detect any sensations there. The awareness then shifts down to the right ear, concentrating there likewise, then to the left ear, nose, eyes, mouth, chin, neck, back of the head, shoulders and down each arm separately to

---

9   Puja means honor, worship and devotional attention. In the context of Buddhism, it is the fact or quality of being devoted to religious observances or a solemn dedication to an object or a person.

the fingertips, then back to the chest and from there to the stomach, hips and into each leg to the toes, focusing all the time on feeling any sensation whatsoever that might be in each area.

Once the ability to feel sensations has become steady and keen, the awareness moves in a more general way, which Goenka called, 'sweeping'. This is done by starting at the top of the head and literally sweeping awareness steadily down through the entire body without stopping at any particular spot to the toes, then immediately returning to the top of the head, where the process starts again or, when advanced, one can sweep from the toes back up through the body to the top of the head. That sweeping is repeating over and over and after sweeping for a while, it can be changed to simply observing and feeling the whole body as a form of changing sensations in a more general way.

About the original *Vipassana* meditation practice in Kanduboda, Rahula wrote in his autobiography:

The teacher then described the actual meditation technique. He explained how I should concentrate on the rising and falling movements of the abdomen during the process of normal breathing. A mental note of 'rising, rising' should be made while breathing in and 'falling, falling' while breathing out. This was to be the primary object of focus while sitting. During the pause between breaths or if the breathing became too faint

145

and unnoticeable, then he said to feel where the knees or buttocks touched the floor and make a mental note of 'touching, touching.' If the mind got caught up in thinking, whereupon awareness of sitting and breathing was obscured or lost, it should be recognized as soon as possible by making a note of 'thinking, thinking,' and then simply return awareness to 'rising, rising,' and 'falling, falling.' If I was disturbed by a loud sound, a mental note of 'hearing, hearing' should be made until the sound went away and then return again to 'rising... falling...' The same mental notice-taking applied to the other sensory stimulations of seeing objects, feeling gross body sensations, smelling and tasting, if and when they occurred. In this practice, only the bare observation of the process itself was important. We were not to try to analyze or make judgments concerning them beyond the initial noting. All together, this was the basic rhythm of contemplation while sitting for one-hour periods several times a day. In between sittings, we were to practice walking meditation which he went on to describe. This was a continuation of the sitting awareness, substituting the movement of the feet for the rising and falling of the abdomen. While lifting one foot, make a note of 'lifting, lifting;' when swinging the foot forward 'swinging, swinging;' and when lowering the foot to the ground 'towering, lowering.' This attention was applied to each step in succession without break, while walking very slowly. The rest was the same concerning the mind's errant thinking and the sensory activities of hearing, seeing, smelling, tasting and touching—giving only bare attention to the initial raw sensory phenomenon.

Since Rahula's interest in *Vipassana* had arisen, he had bought two books in Colombo recommended on the subject. One was *The Heart of Buddhist Meditation* by the Venerable Nyanaponika Thera, a German monk living in Sri Lanka; the other was *Practical Insight Meditation* by Mahasi Sayadaw, a Burmese monk/meditation master. Using the time until the course began, he started reading because he knew that reading books, while on intensive retreat at Kanduboda, was not permitted. He found the texts extremely straightforward and clear; were about the need for mindfulness in our daily lives and the power of mindfulness to uncover the hidden dark recesses of the mind and get rid of the various hindrances to realizing inner peace and eventual Enlightenment. The method of *Vipassana* expounded in both these books was different from Goenka's sweeping.

At the first meeting with Bhante Sivali, and listening to his basic instructions, Rahula found that it coincided with what he had read in the books. Bhante Sivali instructed him further to sit for an hour, if possible, followed by thirty minutes or so of walking meditation and alternating these periods of awareness as much as possible from early morning till night. For the routine activities of the day such as eating, bathing, using the toilet and so on, he said Rahula should slow down all general movements. When he asked Bhante Sivali about the different breathing technique (*Anapanasati*), he told him he had learned from Goenka, namely feeling the breath at the tip of the nose, the teacher replied that the awareness of the rising and falling of the abdomen was itself a form of Anapanasati and more conducive for the cultivation of an alert awareness of insight. Rahula would later leave the decision up to his students how they wanted to feel the breath.

The brief introduction to meditation practice and the advice to slow down all movement sounded familiar to Rahula because this was in the above-mentioned books he had read. He accepted it from the outset as the right induction to the practice. None of his students nowadays would be surprised at this because this is what he has been teaching all along. It was his alternative approach to meditation techniques that seems to have fulfilled the saying 'third time lucky'.

After the *Mahayana* based first meditation course in Nepal and the body-scan practice he learned with Goenka, he has never left this path of meditation since the teaching he was given at Kanduboda, although in his practice and teaching he employs various other useful techniques apart from Yoga. One of these techniques is body scan meditation, which he presents in his meditation courses as just one possible *Vipassana* technique, thereby ignoring Goenka's advise, or rather, his demand that

Vipassana can be taught by using body scan practice only.

That advice was given to him at the end of the course, when Rahula, like all the other students, had a final talk with Goenka. First, he expressed how grateful he was and next conveyed how this sweeping technique had revolutionized his meditation practice. He then said he would like to instruct others in this simple practice, referring specifically to his parents, whereupon Goenka replied it would be okay, but only for close family members, who otherwise would never have any opportunity to practice it. But he demanded, however, that Rahula not change or modify the technique, but explain it exactly as he had taught it, which should be effective enough. This stipulation was not only meant for Rahula but applies to all appointed and authorized teachers of Goenka's *Vipassana* practice, namely to follow his teachings exactly, which is also the policy adopted for student courses worldwide.

Goenka's singularity of focus on body scan meditation stems from his conviction that his technique is the only one that leads to liberation, to enlightenment, and he would therefore not have been content with one of his first student's development regarding meditation technique. However, he would not really have cared and neither of them were to meet again anyway. Nevertheless, Rahula honored

Goenka's teaching, saying he acquired more understanding of the *Dhamma* in the way of the last words of the Buddha, which Goenka recited during the course. They are:

I've expounded the Dhamma in all possible ways, nothing is hidden; take this Dhamma for your refuge; light the lamp of Dhamma within you; don't depend on anyone else to save you. All conditioned things are impermanent; work out your salvation with diligence.

This was the way Rahula was beginning to see and accept as what he had to do. The Goenka course, he told me, was to him like kind of a turning point when he started to shift from *Mahayana* teaching to the more non-verbal development of awareness and concentration expounded in the *Theravada*.

"At the end of that meditation course," he said: "I was kind of convinced I wanted to go to Sri Lanka and study *Vipassana* in more detail. I heard about the different style of *Vipassana* courses and *Vipassana* meditation and that Sri Lanka is a nice place and that people can be ordained there very easily and stay for a long period of time. That's when I gradually cemented the idea of going to Sri Lanka and becoming a monk."

At the same time he was aware of losing the first impressions the Lamas from Nepal had given him with their *Mahayana* based meditation. He wrote about it as follows:

With my growing leanings towards these Theravada

or Hinayana *teachings, I could almost envision Lama Zopa and Lama Yeshe shaking their heads in disapproval, but I couldn't seem to do anything about it.*

A *Vipassana* meditation retreat of ten or fourteen days with Bhante Rahula is not only a chain of periods seated on a meditation cushion supplemented by some Yoga exercises or walking meditation. It also transforms all daily activities into a state of utmost awareness, which he was taught in Kanduboda: a certain schedule is set and, most importantly, one has to give up any communication in order to comply with the so-called Noble Silence, by remaining undisturbed at any time during the retreat and being able to focus on every moment and movement that happens. Maintaining silence is not the only requirement, but also the avoidance of any other form of communication like such as, eye contact, for instance. It might look a little strange when observing such things on the outside and even bear some similarity to what Rahula was thinking in Kanduboda on observing the students already practicing their meditation, pacing with that exaggerated slow motion with their eyes downcast in front of their feet.

"They looked something like walking zombies", he said:

I recall I was a little annoyed on my first retreat by some participants, obviously advanced students, who had already assumed the behavior described above even before the course had begun by not looking at me or even nodding when I greeted them.

Why is it that important not to communicate and focus only on one self? After all, is it not polite to say 'good morning' every day, or to open the door for someone or smile when meeting? Of course it is, but it also brings you away from yourself and what is happening to you at that very moment. However, you are not going to a retreat to show how polite you are (or even observe how impolite your companions might be) but to gain insight into what is really happening.

It cannot therefore do any good to revert to normal, everyday behavior between the sessions. Staying aware even when not sitting or walking in meditation mode is the key to more awareness. The strict schedule is also helpful even if it might not be very convenient to some given that the wakeup time is 4:45 am, but it is a good exercise to observe what is happening to you at that early hour if you are not an 'early bird' type.

Bhante Sivali in Kanduboda described this in his short introduction, that noting every momentary action or perception is supposed to keep the mind on the activity while it is occurring in the present moment and aids in establishing an objective detachment.

"This 'bare attention' is very effective in establishing some mental space to break spontaneous, habitual reactions, both physical and emotional, and the suffering that would normally ensue," Rahula said "during a meditation course, the main assignment for the students is to train their awareness and it is good advice to do it all the time."

I was myself once in Kanduboda as well. After a two-week trip with a Sri Lankan monk I know very well from Germany, the Venerable Bhante Punnaratana, who has founded a charity to aide school projects and other educational facilities. We were traveling around, visiting various projects. After that exciting tour, I spent three nights in peace and quiet at the center before returning home. What I observed there and, of course, becoming part of it, was also what Rahula described in his autobiography. I could see him in my mind's eye: I could imagine him, for example, lining up for breakfast or lunch, slowly walking with his eyes lowered towards the heels of the person in front, observe him taking his seat at the table reserved for lay people with the monks already sitting apart at 'theirs'; I see him turning his head, perhaps thinking: 'turning, turning' or, when looking at his food: 'looking, looking' and, while arranging it: 'arranging, arranging'. Yes, he would have noted all these separate activities in the same manner that I did myself.

He demonstrates it on his retreats and it is without doubt first questionable when he lifts a mug with tea in it to his mouth, saying 'lifting, lifting', takes a sip with 'drinking, drinking', or 'swallowing, swallowing' and the same with eating: lifting the spoon to his mouth with 'lifting, biting', 'lowering' the spoon to the table and then 'chewing, swallowing'. First, the spoon is put down before chewing because it is all about sequential awareness. If you do not do this, you can confuse the awareness of lowering with chewing. Being aware means being present at every given moment with no thoughts about what to do after lunch like taking a nap, going for a walk or whatever else might come into your head—and that such thoughts will come is certain. The only way to stay where you are with your awareness of what is happening right now is to observe where you are and what you are doing and, in order to achieve that, you eat and drink very mindfully, slowing down all your movements.

In walking meditation, you lift a foot, swing it forward, pause a little, lower it and then set it on the ground: lifting, swinging, pausing, lowering and setting are the notable actions. After you have trained yourself properly, you need no longer note your movements or perceptions because you are aware of each one anyway. Only when you notice that you have lost your awareness, can you start noting each movement again until awareness is fully refocused. When the movements are slow enough and your awareness is sharply in focus, the beginning and end—the duration or life-span of each body movement—can be distinguished. One is also aware that every movement is necessarily preceded by an intention from the mind. The body can do nothing on its own.

Rahula recommends training yourself to observe the beginning and end of any movement should not be limited to your time on the retreat. In daily life it might not always be appropriate to slow down for the sake of awareness, but in some cases it is. Let me instance a situation of us are probably familiar with, like standing in a line and waiting. We would not have intended our movements to slow down, yet they do anyway. Think about a line where you are waiting for a train ticket. You can torture yourself with all the (uncomfortable) future possibilities or you can try to be aware of what is happening right now: you stand and wait; 'standing, standing—waiting, waiting'. Some three-part breathing exercises might help. Doing that, sounds better to me than thinking you might be running out of time for a snack before the train leaves, or buying a book, or even wondering whether the schedule time is wrong.

Trying to be aware of what is happening around you, being aware of reality, is not in itself the goal of meditation. Rahula understands such problems and difficulties and his teaching supplies the tools needed to deal with them in daily life.

My first impression of him was, as I have already noted, that he is calm. Knowing him better now, however, I would not longer put it that way. The better word would be 'aware'. He was aware of what he was doing. He lives what he teaches, as I have been able to observe very often since then. Whether in a crowded Home Depot, buying a generator for the monastery when he was the vice abbot there, or meeting him after we had lost each other for almost an hour on a walk through the Grand Canyon, or me informing him on a retreat that the meditation hall had to be closed for the time being because of an up-coming problem with the roof, he was always aware of just what was happening and if something needed managing, as in the last case, it would be, in a thorough and profound way, about the arrangements that had to be made.

Sri Lanka's citizens are mostly Buddhists, but that does not mean you will find a lot of meditation in the thousands of Buddhist temples and centers all over the country. Rahula's observation about the practice of the Sri Lankan Buddhists agreeing with mine, plus what I was told by Sri Lankans themselves, reveals a friendly and compassionate community trying to live faithfully by the five precepts, visiting the temples from time to time, giving *Dana*[10], reciting a few of the traditional Buddhist chants and reading books on meditation or Buddhist philosophy. For most people, it seems to be impossible to attain *Nirvana* in this lifetime, but in a future life they might have the chance to become a monk or a nun and attain enlightenment then, which therefore motivates them to really want to be reborn. Giving *Dana* is the way to do that.

"The deeper purpose of *Dana*," Rahula said, "is to weaken one's grief and therefore self-centeredness."

When one weakens grief, it feels better because the heart becomes more open. It is a natural result. That is why people practice it, and because good *Karma* is involved, pleasant results ensue. *Dana* helps both the giver and the recipient and the nature of the giving falls into three categories: from the giver's point of view, there is kingly giving, friendly giving or beggarly giving.

Beggarly giving is, as Rahula described, when we give with only one hand, still holding onto what we are giving. In this kind of giving, we give the least of what we have and afterwards wonder whether we should have given at all. In friendly giving, we give open-handedly: we

10   Dana is the practice of cultivating the virtue of generosity in Hinduism, Buddhism, Jainism and Sikhism. According to historical records, it is an ancient practice in Indian traditions, tracing back to Vedic traditions.

take what we have and share it because to do so seems appropriate. It is, and when we have enough, it is easy to give. It's a clear kind of giving. In kingly giving, we give the best of what we have, even if nothing remains for ourselves. He went on:

"This, from the Buddhist point of view, is the highest sort of *Dana* because it is not only merely for oneself, but spreads *Dhamma* to bring happiness to the whole world. Of course, it also brings the individual happiness, but that is not the only purpose."

Rahula had chosen Sri Lanka for a reason and he was going to use any occasion that is meeting his expectations and plans. After the course in Kanduboda he had a more profound insight into the practice and merits of meditation. He wanted to practice somewhere, preferably secluded and surrounded by nature. A guy, whom he met in Colombo, recommended the place, where he lived with his girlfriend, and offered shelter at his rented house in Unawatuna, a bay with a large, curved, almost-deserted beach a few miles south of Galle.

The beach is no longer 'almost deserted' nor is Unawatuna a secluded area. Bhante Rahula, who travels and teaches all over the world sometimes has friends and students that have taken the opportunity to travel with him and join his retreats or simply go on excursions with him that he likes so much. With other

158

friends from Germany that I know from the meditation retreats, I took the chance to travel with him on one of his journeys to Sri Lanka and join a *Vipassana* retreat in Nilambe high in the mountains near Kandy. We extended the trip, not only especially for me, to stay with him in some places where he used to live and which I wanted to see for the purpose of this book.

On our way, we also visited Unawatuna. One day I was standing together with Rahula on the coast and it was hard to imagine what he saw when he first set foot on this beach, but he described it to me:

"When I first came in here in 1974, I was walking from the road but there were no hotels here of any kind, just a small village with no traffic on the road. When I came to this opening and looked across the bay to that hill, there was nothing on top of it. That Stupa and the other things weren't there. And there were no boats, nothing, and it was very peaceful and I was just looking at it and it was like I couldn't speak, you know. It was so beautiful, the whole scenery, and I was mesmerized. It was like a déjà vu experience and there I stood looking at it for a long time. Then I walked slowly over to the hill and I wanted to meditate there."

Nowadays, Unawatuna and the beach afford one of the most popular mass tourist spots in that area, which has not only been changed by the buildings along the beach for tourists such as bars and restaurants, but also by the Tsunami in 2004. We were talking about these changes while walking along the beach when Rahula said:

"They just widened that beach and, by doing so, made the water area much smaller. Before, it came out to somewhere like here," and he showed me with his hand and I said:

"Maybe they did it or the sea did by itself."

"No," he said, "they did it. They said it was a Belgian project. The beach had been washed away basically. And that mole wasn't there either."

The sand of the beach actually had two different colors and consistencies, and Rahula added:

"Where the white sand is, that is all new sand. I wonder how they did that," and I said:

"Me too, but it is nice sand. I like the color."

Although the Tsunami destroyed all of the buildings, killed thirteen citizens and swept away the sandy beach, human activities caused the worst. Reconstructing the beach with sand from elsewhere was well intentioned enough, but the mole at the end of the bay has disrupted the natural flow of the currents and also destroyed the beautiful coral reef next to the shore, and then, long before the Tsunami hit, there was this plan to develop a big resort for a foreign hotel chain. For that purpose, they felled most of the mangroves, dredged the soil and filled it with sand. That project never got off the ground, however, maybe because of the Tamil war, which broke out in Sri Lanka in the early 'eighties.

Despite the history of the beach's unfortunate development, we had a laugh about another aspect of its past that Rahula recounted to me about the beach when it was so secluded. I was rather surprised and asked:

"You mean they used the sand as a toilet?"

"Yes. I used to come down from there," he pointed to the hill, "on my alms rounds over the beach and watched all the men taking a shit and using the seawater like in a flush toilet. The tide would come in and whoosh … Sometimes I had to be very careful were I put my feet, you know."

Anyway, what attracted Rahula the most was actually still to be seen: at the base of the hill at the end of the curved palm-fringed beach was a walled enclosure containing a few small yellow buildings. He explained:

"The isolated little compound displayed an air of peaceful tranquility, sitting there all by itself. The picturesque storybook setting stunned me. It felt as though a strong connection had been made in my heart or mind. I could only just stand there with my eyes fixed upon that dreamlike and tempting scene."

He almost immediately checked the spot out.

It is a kind of Hindu-cum-Buddhist temple area where Hindu gods are worshiped. One of the buildings contained a large Buddha statue. Nobody lived there permanently and the buildings were generally kept locked up. It was really nicely located at the foot of a little hill and, for the rest, surrounded by palm trees, the beach and the ocean. A little path leads to and through the village and across the hill. On the other side of the path had lain that mangrove forest, which, alas, was no longer there, but the beauty of the compound, the beach and ocean and the hill that had so deeply impressed Rahula, remained. I could imagine how that very place must have appeared while standing with him there thirty-two years later.

He was, one could say, so infatuated with it that he and his friend Chris, an Englishman who had joined him at the Kanduboda retreat and had been traveling with him since, decided to try to reside in or around the compound. It seemed the perfect spot for deep meditation. From a villager he met at the place, he learned that he had to go for permission to a monk, who was in charge of this, at the local village Buddhist temple. This local temple is still there. A little hidden to the right of the road when coming from the country road and after passing almost all of the tourist bars, shops, and restaurants. We visited it on my way with Bhante Rahula. The first impression could not be ignored: a lot of dogs started barking when we walked through the (open) gate. For me it was a little scary, but Rahula seemed unimpressed. He pointed at the dogs and said:

"Every year there are one or two more."

We met the Venerable Ariyajothi and he invited us into the building—not because of the dogs, who still were barking away but, as he said:

"The mosquitos coming."

It was, by the way, the same monk who later gave Rahula permission to build a Kuti. A Kuti is the living place, separated in the monasteries from the sacred buildings, in which the monks live, sleep and meditate. When I talked to Ariyajothi about the Kuti and the permission he gave Rahula to build it, he said:

"That young western monk seemed to be very responsible."

Rahula had erected that Kuti on the hill behind the Devale, which is what the temple area was called, in 1980.

Back in 1974, it was a different monk he had to ask. At that time Rahula was a lay person. As far as the monk was concerned, he was a tourist with an interest in meditation, but he gave him permission, to use the Devale, and also the key to the Buddha shrine. Perhaps Rahula also made the same impression on that monk.

In 1974, there were not so many Westerners seen around and Rahula and Chris made quite a spectacle when walking through the village. People came to their doors and watched them curiously. They would see a lot more of them both in the future, especially Rahula, because he liked the beauty of the beach and the ocean, the Devale with the hill behind and the village from the very beginning. He knew the area here was one of a kind.

"Being here," he said, "was like a dream come true and I couldn't help but ponder over the *Karma* that brought me to this secluded paradise. I was sitting on a deserted beach in the midst of probably the most beautiful seacoast landscape I had ever laid eyes on, blissed out of my skull—and all without drugs."

Then he told me what happened the next day after Chris and he had settled in, spending their time in meditation, Yoga exercises and sleeping on their bedrolls under the eave behind the Buddha shrine. In the morning they awoke before sunrise and were starting the day with meditation, Yoga sessions and reading the books Rahula had bought in Colombo about different Buddhism topics.

They were seated in their second meditation session when it happened. Rahula heard noises of people that were clearly coming towards them. He said:

"I tried to put it out of my mind with 'hearing,

hearing' but that didn't work so well. They came right into the hallway and stopped a few feet away from us, whispering among themselves and placing things on a table which was in the corner. I was curious to find out what was going on. So I slowly raised one of my eyelids to take an inconspicuous peek and found them looking right into my eye. I quickly shut the eye again to think about it. There were two old women, one man and two children with a few baskets on the table. It was quite obvious that they wanted our attention and I knew it would do no good to try and ignore them by pretending to be in oblivious *Samadhi*. They now knew I was conscious of their presence. The meditation hour was almost up anyway, so I opened both eyes and shot a glance at Chris, who seemed to be waiting for me to make the first move. The people were busying themselves taking plates, bowls and containers of food out of the baskets, and I soon realized that they wanted to offer us a meal. None of them spoke English and in my few broken words of Sinhalese, along with some sign language, I tried to make it known that the two of us did not desire to eat, that we were fasting. I thought maybe they had the mistaken impression that we were monks, so I pointed to our hair and my bushy beard, saying, 'No monks, no monks.'"

It was hopeless. These simple villagers could not understand Rahula's futile explanation, or else they did not believe it, or they simply did not care. To them, he and his friend, Chris, had to eat, whether they were monks or not; it did not matter. The plates were becoming piled high with rice and curries. It was too late.

"Chris and I looked at each other with puzzled expressions," Rahula said, "and I told him that to be polite we might as well break our fast and eat some of it so as not to hurt their feelings."

They appeared to be sincere and devoted Buddhists, whoever they were, and the two old ladies were fussing over getting everything ready. They prepared a small plate of food, which was offered to the Buddha, as is the custom before serving monks, and they knelt down in front of the altar chanting the appropriate stanzas for this act of merit. When everything was ready, they offered glasses of water, which they had also brought along for washing their hands and drinking, and then they handed them the plates heaped with food.

"Then," Rahula said, "the ladies stepped back and held their hands in the respectful Namaskar as if waiting for us to say something in response. I did not know the proper kind of merit transference and blessings that the monks traditionally recite so I said, "bohoma stuti" (thank you very much). They seemed to get a kick out of my few words of Sinhalese and they smiled and watched on, waiting for us to begin eating. I wanted to eat enough to make it worth their effort coming all the way out here carrying the heavy baskets. After I indicated that I had had enough, the man who had been standing idly around brought us a bowl of water to wash our soiled fingers. Now, as if all this was not enough, the man pulled out a thermos bottle along with cups and saucers. I thought to myself, 'My God, tea or coffee too?' Yep, they served us each a cup of sweetened black coffee; I suppose to aid digestion. The full course 'beggars banquet' was now complete and they began packing all of the leftovers and dirty dishes back into the baskets."

When the small group had left, Chris and Rahula discussed the incident, trying to figure it out. The only explanation was that the word must have leaked out that two foreign Yogis were dwelling in the Devale, practicing Yoga and meditation. Thinking they had nothing to eat, these caring villagers had taken it upon themselves to feed them.

In the late afternoon, a villager named Eustace had heard about the two western Yogis. There was obviously a village gossip grapevine. He spoke relatively good English and came to visit them. Asked about the *Dana* that had been given, he explained that these simple people and devoted Buddhists had heard that two foreigners had just arrived and what they know about real meditation was that it is the way to attain *Nirvana*. They made it their duty as Buddhists to support them as they would anyone else trying earnestly to achieve the goal of liberation. It would be a great merit for them if a person did attained Enlightenment supported by their *Dana*. Eustace confirmed that it did not matter that neither of them were monks. The villagers were kind of thrilled that Westerners had come halfway around the globe and, in their eyes, sacrificed so much to take up, in such primitive conditions, the Buddha way. He said a lot of the local families would probably be anxious to offer them *Dana*.

I think and I said to Rahula: it is a little bit strange for Buddhist people in the East that do not practice meditation so much to experience Buddhists from the West that do. From his own observations that he had made then and later he had this to say about it:

"In Sri Lanka, as in some other eastern countries, people grow up being Buddhist with the doctrines like rebirth and *Karma* already laid out for them. These are already taught these things when they're young and they are already Buddhists in the same way as we grow up as Christians. So we think we are Christians and they think they are Buddhists and that's that. They know what the Buddha does and learn the rituals from their parents and a little bit about the doctrine without really going that deep into it. They hear about meditation, but the monks and other people around them do not really practice it and, as a result, never give them the incentive to do so either. So the majority of the people try to practice so that they get reborn into the future life. *Dana* is the big thing for them if they are good at that. They like to give and practice *Sila* to some extent, but they don't meditate. They are kind of *Dana-Sila* Buddhists. And rituals are important for them: having monks bless their baby or bless a new house; employing rituals to kind of avoid evil spirits and practicing *Metta*[11]. Being a decent, benevolent person is the aim, but the meditation aspect is kind of lacking. In western countries it is somewhat to the contrary. Most Westerners have already either rejected or lapsed from the religion of their birth. Most Christians or Jews do not seriously practice their religion. If they come into contact with Buddhist teaching, they immediately appreciate the aspect of meditation. For most of them, suffering psychologically, the use of it is to find an inner

11   Metta, is an essential part of Buddhism The Pali word is meaning loving-kindness, friendliness or good-will. It is defined as the strong wish for the welfare and happiness of others (parahita-parasukha-kamana). True metta is devoid of self-interest. It evokes within a warm-hearted feeling of fellowship, sympathy and love, which grows boundless with practice and overcomes all social, religious, racial, political and economic barriers. Metta is indeed a universal, unselfish and all-embracing love.

peace and understanding. So they are more in meditation and not so much into rituals, not necessarily devotion to *Buddha, Dhamma, Sangha*. Some of them might not even call themselves Buddhists."

"By the way," I said, "there is a question whether Buddhism is a religion at all."

"If Buddhism is a religion, it depends on what you make out of it. You can make it a religion or you can make it your way of life. And it depends on what you call religion. Some people say, I don't know what the dictionary says, religion is something built around a god. If that is what you mean by religion, then Buddhism is not a religion. But if religion for you means some way to open up and transcend the self and the experiences, something beyond the body and mind, regardless of what you call it, when that is what you mean by religion, then Buddhism would also be a religion. But I know for myself what it is; that is, when I call it religion, then it is. But I don't. The common belief is that Buddhism is considered a religion. We don't have to tell people, no, it is not a religion; we have to explain properly what it means. Religion is just a word. Any word is just a word. But the meaning, what it means to you is what is important. My father took me to the Methodists. I was a churchgoer until I went to high school, which means until about the age of sixteen. I still might have gone a few times later. We had a church group that was for youth, so I didn't actually go to church for the services, I went to the youth group. We studied a little bit about Christianity, but mostly it was just for social things, you know, we met a lot of girls, there were a lot of activities, outings, stuff like that."

"A good point," I said. "For me there has always been this difference to other religions and so I don't call Buddhism that, first of all because there is no god and, secondly, because the Buddha doesn't demand followers."

"Not blindly believing ones, yes. You have to test the *Dhamma* for yourself and if you find it good and useful, then follow it. You do it on your own. The demand to follow is a kind of control over people."

Buddhism, when considered as a religion, might be hard to define. What it became to Rahula and what he later was going to spread with his teaching, he stated in an interview that he gave on the occasion of the twentieth anniversary of the Bhavana forest monastery in West Virginia in 2009:

Buddhism is a kind of a self help practice using the tools of meditation and the tools of what the Buddha taught, the Noble Eightfold Path. We can act to start to change our life, change the way we think, and overcome some bad habit that we might have, and also find a new way of relating to the world that brings us a deeper kind of tranquility.

Over the next six weeks, after they settled at the Devale, the routine continued with meditation and sunrise Yoga. Different groups of villagers faithfully brought lunch each day, and many mornings someone would bring breakfast as well.

Since it was a public shrine, people would come to worship and perform Pujas from time to time anyway, sometimes arriving in big tour parties. Several people came with the sole intention of meeting and speaking. There were also regular visits from Eustace and, in some conversations with him and a few others, the subject came up of Chris and Rahula officially becoming real monks.

This idea was not new to Rahula. It had sometimes been more, sometimes less hidden in the back of his mind since the meditation course at Kopan and became a more conscious idea after Kanduboda. Since arriving at Unawatuna, however, he had all but forgotten about it and was content to live as he was, which was almost a monk's life anyway. Now that the subject had been brought up again, he realized that he had no incentive left to revert to ordinary life nor to go around the world looking for different experiences.

With this renewed discussion on the topic, and all the physical requirements for such a move near at hand, he realized that he was probably ready. His companion, Chris, was not so sure, but the idea of becoming a monk appealed to his manner of "let's try and see."

Having both of them as real monks would mean a lot to the villagers, who were supporting them so diligently, and provide them with great status. Eustace enthusiastically described how there would be a big procession with them riding on elephants through the village and along the Galle/Matara road complete with the whole traditional ceremony.

If he was to ordain at all, Rahula thought, why not give these kind-hearted people the opportunity to share actively in it? Eustace knew the high priest of a big temple a few miles away. So one day early in the morning, they all walked the three or four miles to it. Besides being a temple, it acted as a school or training center for about twenty young novice monks studying for the higher priesthood.

The Chief Incumbent, who spoke no English, told Eustace that he was delighted to hear that both of these Westerners had been living at the Devale, but actually he had already been apprised of this. Their desire to ordain now seemed to make him happy. However, they were foreigners and he was not sure of the procedure. He would need some time to think it over.

A few days later, he regretfully informed them that he could not grant them ordination. He was not sure of the government's policy towards admitting foreigners to the *Sangha*. He did not have the proper facilities either and communication would be difficult. He explained that new monks were supposed to stay with their preceptor or teacher generally for a least five years to receive training in the proper monks' etiquette (code of discipline), memorizing scriptural passages, learning Pali and studying the ancient texts.

Neither Rahula nor Chris were much interested in that anyway. They mainly wanted to continue their own meditative lifestyle at the Devale. Nonetheless, it was then about two weeks before their visas expired and they would have to return to Colombo to obtain another two months' extension.

In Colombo, they got the recommendation to go to Kandy. It was the place where the famous German monk and author of *The Heart of Buddhist Meditation*, the Venerable Nyanaponika, lived in a hermitage in the forest. Rahula was keen on visiting him. Nyanaponika lived in a big house outside the city and Rahula took a walk there that he described as delightful.

"Bands of monkeys," he said, "freely roamed through the stands of straight tall vine covered trees and a large pond bordered by giant bamboos and overhanging trees with vines trailing down made it look like something out of a Tarzan movie."

Nyanaponika, who, by the way, is considered the most outstanding translator of Buddhist texts into German, plus his having been the teacher of Bhikkhu Bodhi, who is considered the same for his translations into English, was busy with writing and editing when Rahula arrived. Nevertheless, he was kind enough to welcome him in and sit and converse with him for a while.

From him, Rahula got a recommendation to another meditation center like the one in Kanduboda, the Gothama Thapovanaya. Nyanaponika told him that the English of the teacher, Venerable Vangisa Maha Thera, was not so good, but he gave instructions through a translator.

Besides Thapovanaya was the only other meditation center that catered to Westerners and it was conveniently located just six miles outside Colombo in a rubber forest. With that information, Rahula knew what to do before leaving for India and the Yoga course. Chris, who was recovering from an infection he had contracted in Unawatuna, decided to stay in Kandy until the 28th of September, the departure date for the Yoga course in Pondicherry, India.

In Thapovanaya, Rahula encountered the identical *Vipassana* method that he had learned at Kanduboda and the set-up and organization were similar. When, after a month, he had finished the course, he was

175

more or less in the same mood to join the monkhood as he had been when returning from India.

Chapter 8

"To worry is to become accessible, unwittingly accessible. And once you worry you cling to anything out of desperation; and once you cling you are bound to get exhausted or to exhaust whoever or whatever you are clinging to." These words are from the book *Journey to Ixtlan* by Carlos Castaneda. He was an American writer and especially famous for a series of books about the teaching of the Mexican 'Indian' shaman named Don Juan. The texts are related to experiences with peyote and other psychotropic drugs. Rahula read the first two books of the series, as I mentioned earlier, during his 'seeking phase' in Amsterdam when he was there with Barry and Fred, his old school mates from Riverside. The third book, *Journey to Ixtlan* he acquired accidentally when he was back in Gothama Thapovanaya after finishing the Yoga course in India.

With his *Vipassana* experience, he could see similarities with the knowledge of reality taught by the Mexican sorcerer, Don Juan.

Rahula said that the passages describing the 'Path of a Warrior' and the 'warrior's' ability to perform 'not doing' in order to 'stop the world' and 'see', thus becoming a 'person of knowledge' seemed to hit the nail right on the head. In *Vipassana*, the yogi accomplishes 'not doing' by cultivating unhindered attention and 'stops the world' by applying clear comprehension, cultivating equanimity and experiencing 'cessation'. Hence, he or she becomes a 'person of knowledge' or in Buddhist terms, an Enlightened One. The title *Journey to Ixtlan* is a metaphor to describe the predicament that faces a warrior, meditator, or spiritual seeker. Ixtlan represents the conditioned illusory world—our ideals, identity, self-image, family, home, country, etcetera. Everyone is on that journey, hoping to reach, to arrive, to hold onto and protect one's idea of happiness and security in this impermanent world.

After the Yoga course in India, Rahula went back to the temple Gothama Thapovanaya, where he and the Venerable Vangisa Maha Thera had a laugh when the monk said he was pleased that Rahula had not been led astray by Hinduism. It was, as a matter of fact, rather the contrary. It was, in the words of Carlos Castaneda's text from *Journey to Ixtlan*, similar to the way a meditator gains the knowledge of No-Self or Emptiness. Everything that was considered real and familiar is seen in a whole new perspective. The futility of self-centered striving and craving is understood. Such a person can never go back to the old habitual patterns in the same blind way. Rahula, in the spring of 1975, knew he would never again live an ordinary life, clinging to whatever it would offer him. No sensory indulgence, entertainment or ego gratification. Unlike his recent companion, Chris, who did not return, Rahula would from now on walk the solitary meditative path, to purify his mind of greed, hatred, and delusion with no other duty or obligation except to walk down that path to become 'a man of knowledge'.

He renewed his desire to join the *Sangha*. The Venerable Vangisa was pleased to hear this and happy to lead and supervise him in the process. The ordination ceremony was set for very soon, actually on the Vesak night of the full moon.

Of course, only his noviciate initiation would be undergone at this time. It would act as a training or adjustment period to prepare him psychologically for the higher Bhikkhu ordination and a more austerely committed life. A novice is required to observe only the ten standard precepts plus seventy-five training rules which deal with matters such as how to wear the robes properly, conduct oneself in the monastery and in public, respect the elder monks and so on. But it was Rahula's absolute intention to become a fully ordained Bhikkhu, which would require observing 227 rules and govern just about every aspect of his life. This rigid code of discipline, called the *Vinaya*, was to help keep the aspirant mindful and alert to every activity of the body, speech, and mind, in order to avoid accumulating unwholesome, spiritually obstructing thoughts and habits.

Part of the preparation was to find a monkish name for him. Rahula was hoping to be able to retain the name 'Rahul' but was afraid his teacher would select a special name for him. The name 'Rahul' (in Pali 'Rahula') was given to him at the end of the Yoga course in Pondicherry by Swami Gitananda. Rahula decided to take a Yogi name as a token remembrance of his unofficial discipleship. Without telling Vangisa where he had gotten the idea, he mentioned the name Rahula and, to his great surprise, he heard his teacher say:

"Rahula, Rahula, Lord Buddha's son – yes, that will be a very good name."

But there was also the necessity to have an identifying prefix in order to distinguish him from other monks having the same name. There were many with such common names, such as Ananda, the Buddha's cousin and disciple, and Rahula, the Buddha's son. In Sri Lanka, every Buddhist monk used the name of his native town or village, so the idea of 'American', 'Riverside', or 'California' Rahula were suggested, but found no favor with Rahula himself, who wanted to cut off all such associations as far as possible. His preceptor then suggested the prefix 'Yogavacara'. It is an epithet used by the Buddha for the forest dwelling Bhikkhus, who were devoted to striving to attain the goal of meditation. Rahula liked it and said about it:

"The full name 'Yogavacara Rahula' had a nice ring to it that I could relate to. Having the word Yoga included seemed to fit my particular blend of *Vipassana* meditation and the Yoga practice that I was doing."

At 8 am on the Vesak full moon, the Venerable Vangisa summoned Rahula to his cottage, where he performed the ritual tonsuring by snipping off the first lock of hair accompanied by the instruction to reflect on the impermanence of hair and the rest of the body while chanting the Pali words for hair, teeth, skin, and nails. One of the other monks then shaved his head down to the bare scalp with a sharp, straight razor. This was the first time Rahula had had his head shaved. He had shaved off his beard, by the way, by himself beforehand. He knew it would have to go sooner or later and he was prepared to let go the last vestige of his former hippie image. However, it felt somewhat strange, and for a few days he continued habitually to reach up to stroke his beard. After saying that, he added:

"Even though it wasn't there, I gave my chin a rub anyway."

His shaven head felt pleasantly cool and comfortable and he guessed it was a feeling that would become second nature to him.

Normally a big crowd of devotees came to Gothama Thapovanaya for the monthly full moon Poya (holiday) program. At Vesak, the highest holiday would attract a huge gathering anyway. However, there were about a thousand people expected at this particular Vesak, since, as Rahula had previously discovered, it happened that his ordination, with the presence of dignitaries, including the ambassador of the United States, had been in the newspapers.

The ceremony started, when Rahula followed a line of seven Bhikkhus headed by the Venerable Vangisa into the hall and took his seat on a cushion on the floor in front of the elaborate altar especially erected for the occasion. He glanced around and saw the hall was packed full with a single row of chairs in front, on which sat several western VIPs. A couple of men were moving big lights around and one was shouldering a large movie camera, trying to find the best position.

About the actual ordination procedure, Rahula wrote: *I began by my offering a tray of flowers, incense, and lighting an oil lamp at the feet of the large Buddha statue on the altar ... then remained kneeling before my preceptor. With joined palms, I recited the Pali formula requesting the teacher to grant me out of compassion the Going Forth (Pabbaja) novice ordination. This translated to the effect that I was a suffering soul and wished to liberate myself from the thralls of ignorance, greed, and hatred by being admitted to the Holy Order. I repeated this request three times, following the instructions and promptings I had been given. The preceptor answered by saying he would have compassion on me and grant the request ... All the while camera lights were blaring and the film was rolling; many individual flashbulbs clicked. At this point I stood up, clutching the robes to my bosom and slowly, with head downcast, walked out of the hall to a nearby building where, with the help of a few of the young monks, I donned the saffron robes for the first time. I was literally helpless in the art of wearing the large outer robe which had to be wrapped around the body and draped over the left shoulder while leaving the right shoulder bare. I had difficulty in keeping the robe up over the shoulder; it kept wanting to slide off. When I thought I had it all together, I mindfully headed back to the hall hoping for God's sake that the robe would not fall down in front of everyone. As soon as I re-entered the hall, a thunderous chorus of "Sadhu! Sadhu! Sahdu!" went up and the bright camera lights beamed squarely onto me. I was noticeably (for myself) nervous and with downcast eyes, remaining highly conscious of the robe, I returned to center stage while the lights, camera flashes and exclamations of Sadhus followed. I tried to concentrate on each step so as not to be distracted by all the sensational attention.*

When I reached my space in front of the preceptor, I again knelt down and with joined palms requested the Three Refuges and Ten Precepts. This was the traditional formula for consecrating the Going Forth. Having repeated the vows after my teacher and paying obeisance again to all the robed Sangha members, I sat back down on my cushion facing the glaring lights and the capacity crowd. The Venerable Vangisa then delivered a talk in Sinhala explaining the meaning of ordination and how I came to Gothama Thapovanaya to practice Vipassana Bhavana under him and subsequently desired to renounce the world. He told the audience that it was a difficult thing for a Westerner to renounce the world and become a Buddhist monk because it was alien to Western belief. We would most likely be branded as heretics, escapists or freaks in our own country, even by family and friends; it would also be very difficult to find support for a Bhikkhu living in the West ... The whole time the Thera was speaking, the audience sat in rapt attention, while I was trying to suppress tears of emotion, center myself and struggle to remember the details of my own speech.

Some aspects from this speech were that he, apart from other things, came from a Judaic-Christian background within the Western culture, which is for the most part entirely externally and materialistically oriented, where happiness is primarily based on the objective world. Then he mentioned that when he was growing older and experiencing more of life, including three years in the army and using drugs, something inside him began to become disenchanted at an unconscious level. He thought there must be more to life than this—thoughts that eventually led him to leave his home in California on a tour around the world in order to experience a wider variety of cultures, peoples and religions. He explained that this unconscious spiritual yearning finally led him to Nepal, where his heart and mind opened to the *Dhamma* and since then had been delving into it, trying to penetrate its subtler aspects. He had learned that there is a potential within each being which will sooner or later lead to the spiritual path. He was lucky, he said, that this potential in himself had led to the course that his life had taken and was taking as dependent on and conditioned by the accumulated experiences, actions (*Karma*) of body, speech and mind from past lives and this current life to date, that becoming a monk was just part of the conditioned process, a phase in life taken to find the most direct, perhaps most conducive way. He concluded with an analogy, saying it was "like rain water coursing down a mountainside to reach the final resting place: *Nirvana*".

Is it necessary to become a monk or nun in order to attain this? No, it is not. What is needed to attain enlightenment or *Bodhi*, as it is called in Pali, which means awakening by understanding the *Dhamma*, is the Buddhist teaching. This is (only) set by the Noble Eightfold Path. There is no barring anyone from ‚walking' this path. With the Enlightenment, the *Samsara*, the cycle of existence, ends. The 'final resting place' is reached: the liberation from this imprisonment, the *Nirvana*. If one is on the path, he or she ceases to harbor the 'will to live', which must not be confused with the will to end life or suicide. On the contrary, suicide, to the Buddhist understanding, brings one away from one's life as a human being, which is the requirement for attaining enlightenment in the first place. The 'will to live' is rather something that is inherited in all living beings. Attaining enlightenment and *Nirvana* bursts through the cycle of existence and that 'will to live'.

Every lay person can easily decide to give it up, but the practice of attaining enlightenment is not that easy at all. Dealing with the power of the ego, with attachments, desires and aversions in common daily life is a great challenge, let alone being so mindful as simply to be aware of these things anyway. Mindfulness is indeed the main thing missing in daily life, with all its errands to run, with its tensions, duties, and longings. It also takes a lot of courage and will-power to sit meditating regularly for a whole hour or more.

For the importance of mindfulness, Bhante Rahula's students hear him say in his retreats:

"Mindfulness is the path to the deathless. Unmindfulness is the path to death. The mindful do not die; the unmindful are as if dead already".

186

The Asian *Theravada* Buddhist people that believe enlightenment is only possible in an ordained person's life are understandable. And what of the West, where Buddhism has become a serious practice for a lot of people? Do they expect things to be otherwise or might their expectation at a deep level be the same? Imagine sitting in a car and waiting for the green traffic light and thinking it is always red for you. Even though you may have meditated an hour in the morning, it is not what reality is about. Or waiting in a line at a supermarket check-out just to buy something quickly that is missing from your preparations for dinner. The reality is that you have to wait. Your perception that your line is the slowest is because you are in a hurry. Daily life is full of thoughts in the mind every second of the day and most of them do not deal with the present moment. Mindfulness in the sense of the *Dhamma* does not meet the demands that people in the West have to deal with. It mostly only works on occasions, like during a meditation retreat. That does not mean attaining enlightenment is impossible, but it might prove very unpromising in common daily life. However, the practice fulfills the aspiration considering the karmic effect anyway.

Becoming a monk or a nun means indeed no other duties or obligations other than working only on breaking the cycle of existence, becoming enlightened, although they have to work anyway. However, this is supposed to be carried out with mindfulness instead of making a career or money, caring for a family or taking care of people, somebody or indeed anything at all.

The Noble Eightfold Path is divided into three foundational practices, *Sila* (Ethical Conduct), *Samadhi* (Concentration), and *Prajna* (Wisdom).

Sila is a code of conduct that embraces a commitment to harmony and self-restraint with the principal motivation being non-violence, or freedom from causing harm. The three steps are: Right Speech, Right Action, Right Livelihood

Samadhi means the mind and soul are in equal balance. It is the last of the eight elements of the Noble Eightfold Path: Right Effort, Right Mindfulness and Right Concentration.

With Prajna comes the Right Understanding and Right Intention, the first two elements of the Noble Eightfold Path, the insight into the true nature of reality, namely *Anicca* (Impermanence), *Dukkha* (Suffering), *Anatta* (No-Self).

Although all elements are equal in their practical significance, there is one, as Bhante Rahula told me on one of our walks, that is more evident:

"Without Right Understanding who can practice the other elements of the Path? Right

Understanding has three levels. First you hear, and that might motivate you to practice, and then as you practice, you go on thinking about it, observing, and then you understand once more; finally you have the realization that comes through deep meditation. Without Right Understanding, who would bother to do these things?"

"So," I asked, " Right Understanding is crucial?"

"Of course. You get it happening gradually at the unconscious level; not really in my case, however, because I didn't know anything about the Four Noble Truths intellectually. But then, when I heard of them, I started thinking. Only then did everything else I had done previously fall into place; structure, you know, was given to whatever I might have been thinking about or doing before. Finally, it affords a kind of structure because the human mind is made in a way that needs that logic and structure—that is the way it thinks."

When Rahula knew the date of his ordination, he thought he had to write a few letters, especially to break the news to his parents, family and old friends. He guessed the news would really blow the minds of the whole Riverside gang. On the morning of the ordination ceremony, Rahula got a telegram from a friend in Colombo who had put him up when he was in town, which brought tears to his eyes: "We'll be with you—tuning in on channel

LSD at *Joshua Tree* on Full Moon—Love, Barry, Larry, Fred and other friends."

But what about his parents? From his few letters in the recent past, they knew that he was serious about Yoga and meditation practice, but they had never had a hint at any such drastic move as ordination. He said, thinking back: "I figured the news would freak them out a bit, but they would get over it as they had with my escapades in Afghanistan."

His mother told me she cried when she got the letter, and said: "It was weird. But he invited us to come to Sri Lanka and wrote, 'let me show you what is important in my life.'" His mother did—not go over on that occasion, but a year later—and told me:

"Then I understood".

Concerning the significance of being a monk, she knew only what she had read or heard and admitted that she had understood very little about Buddhism in general until her son explained it to her when she came to Sri Lanka. She stayed in the monastery for almost two weeks and said that all the people there were Buddhists and were very nice.

It was a kind of shock for her, she said, when she first saw someone bowing in front of her son, because she had known him when he had left as this hippie—and now this. A special moment for her was when she met him at the airport for the first time after almost five years. He had informed her beforehand that, as a monk, he was not supposed to be touched. It was strange for her to see him, her youngest son, and she wanted to hug him, but she could not—and did not because she did not want to embarrass him.

"I was not happy when he was going to India in the first place," she said. "I knew India had a lot of strife and trouble. They had a lot of disease and a lot of people. But I could not hold him back. Becoming a monk was not what I wanted for him, and to be alone in his life without a wife and children was a little pity and, I thought, hard for him. But I understood it and then I accepted it. And I felt much better when I got back from Sri Lanka, because I think I understood more about Buddhism and I have a deep feeling about it. If I wasn't a Christian, I figured, I could be a Buddhist."

I asked her, when she returned from Sri Lanka, if she had talked to the other relatives, to her husband and siblings and about their reaction.

"Of course I did. And because I understood and accepted it, they did too. And they still do."

I talked to Rahula's mother in Riverside, California. She was then ninety-seven years old, very lively and alert. She was still driving her car and volunteered one day a week at the information desk in the local hospital.

She now has six grandchildren, six great-grandchildren and five great-great-grandchildren. It is quite a big family and having one son being a monk does not mean he is excluded from family life. Actually, compared with common family life and gatherings, there is not such a big difference. The children having their own families and living elsewhere, the gatherings are mostly limited to birthdays and holidays. Since returning to the USA, Rahula has maintained personal contact with his parents, and since his father died, has continued to do so with his mother and his siblings and their family members as well. Although his sister, Sharon, lives in Arizona and no longer wants to travel so much because it is about a 400-mile drive to her mother's house, her visits are rare, limited to special occasions like their mother's 90th birthday, when the whole family came together. Contact nowadays with her is confined to the regular weekly phone calls his sister makes to her mother and whenever Rahula visits Riverside. However, the relationship with her brother suffers from geographical distance rather than reservations about his becoming a Buddhist monk. Her mother told me that the family accepted Rahula's decision, although this is not entirely the case when it comes to his sister, who, as Rahula told me, had had something of a problem with it.

"She was a kind of Christian fundamentalist

for a long time", he said. "She still is, but she's no longer kind of fanatical about it anymore. I guess it's because she's getting older. But she believes in the Judgment Day and that anybody who doesn't believe in Jesus is considered to be kind of going to hell."

With his brother, Tom, who is an electronics engineer and currently working for a laser technology company, he has that relationship that brothers might have when living far away from each other anyway. At least since Rahula has been back from Asia, he visits his mother regularly on holidays or other occasions and with his brother living in Riverside, he sees him, his wife and children as well. There is a nephew and also two nieces and when I asked Rahula, if any of his family members were interested in Buddhism, he told me that one of the nieces and his brother had come to a couple of his meditation programs, but they were not really into it. His brother, who also likes to hike, as all the DuPrez children were brought up to do so by their parents during childhood, took the chance to accompany Rahula recently on a four week hiking trek in the Himalaya area. It was the first time in about forty-five years that the brothers had spent so much time together.

So Rahula as a monk still has his family life on occasions and especially nowadays, as his mother is getting older, he tries to be less far away from her. She herself had pitied him for not being able to have his own family life, to have married and had children, but she still has a son at least and she is at peace with his decision to become a Buddhist monk. The only thing still disturbing her is that, as she told me: "I can't hug him."

Trekking for Rahula is one of his favorite activities and liking it is for him at one with the spiritual practice embedded in it. He did and still does, after his first attraction to the Himalayas in 1973, hike in the area. Based on an extended tour undertaken in 1999, *The Great Himalayan Traverse* as it was called, he wrote a travel book with a lot of photos in it. In his foreword, he wrote, apart from other things: *For a Buddhist, spiritual practice means purifying the underlying forces of attachment/greed, aversion/hatred, and the selfish ego/delusion in one's mind. It weakens the habitual patterns of clinging to security (as the known), of fearing the unknown and of protecting the ego's boundaries. It is also the cultivation of compassion and loving kindness for oneself and all beings. I know of no better place to do all that than on the trails of the Himalaya(s) in India.*

A Himalayan trek is a metaphor for life itself. On a trek we are searching for a majestic peak or high plateau, a beautiful stream or waterfall, or a shrine or monastery. The destination or goal serves to quench our thirst, our desire. It provides a short respite from the rigors of the trail, a brief "One Night's Shelter." Then we have to descend, move on. We cannot stay there. ... The Himalaya(s) are your own mind. When

194

you have traversed the peaks and valleys, going beyond pleasure and pain, gain and loss, like and dislike, explored the caves of sadness, loneliness, fear, unfulfilled hopes, walked the slippery slopes of desire and lust, pride and conceit, and ultimately crossed the glacier of the ego, this is the end of the trail.

But the hiking trips are not limited to the Himalayan area. On his journeys, although they are undertaken mostly for teaching purposes, he uses the occasions to explore the area around or go to interesting places located nearby. If there are mountains, all the better. For him, out in a forest, it is easy to just forget himself and imagine he is simply another plant, another tree. When he is able to walk and feel the sensations of his body, whether it is aching muscles, his heart beating or his breathing—these all being natural vibrations and connecting with the natural vibrations in the warmth of the sun, the wind and the sound of a stream—all this helps him to bring unity to the experience of consciousness.

Even when the group decision was to take a bus, as on the occasion of crossing the Kunzum pass (some 15,060 feet above mean sea level), he felt the desire to get out and walk the remaining distance to the peak. The scenery, he said, was too beautiful, too immense to be enjoyed while being cooped up in a rattling bus and he told the others not to wait; he would catch up with them at the lake.

"Yes," he said, "it might not be the common preference, but I like to feel the earth under my feet, not the bumps of shock absorbers. I like to feel the cool breeze or sun's rays on my body, not the smell of sweat or hot air inside a crowded bus, with their drivers and (guides?) chain smoking while driving. I like to hear the sounds of bubbling streams, the singing of the birds and the rustle of leaves in the trees rather than the sounds of roaring engines and the rattling of metal, glass and bones; then I am no longer divided and it is beautiful when nature outside connects with the nature of my body."

He is, as he was in that above example, not always alone on his hiking tours, although he "actually prefers going alone", because he invites students and friends to join him in that kind of meditative and spiritual practice. I know a couple of students that were with him on tours, for example around Mount Kailash in western Tibet that I myself skipped because of the height. I had already had problems with breathing in Cuzco, Peru, which is only about 11,200 feet in altitude while you can hike up to about 16,000 feet on Mount Kailash (the peak is actually at 21,778 feet). One woman from Berlin I know from our House of Silence meditation retreats actually lost her mind one day on the trip, asking where she was and needing treatment. Fortunately there was a physician present, our friend Klaus Habich, another regular from Bhante Rahula's retreats, so it was no problem. Plus, to Bhante Rahula, the sickness is part of the awareness of realizing what is happening to your body if it is confronted with an unknown or strange environment. For him every sensation, perception, and irritation is real and can be used as a tool for practice, let alone the aching caused by a longer period of sedentary meditation. One is not supposed in that case to expend energy thinking, like asking oneself when the irritation will cease or even changing one's position to get rid of it. Reality consists in the perception and the impermanence of the sensations.

Becoming aware of the impermanence of all that happens within and around us is one of the cornerstones of his teaching, based on the observation of what is happening in every single moment in order to get to know reality. He teaches it because he practices it. It was his vision of his lifestyle as a mendicant monk, "dwelling in this or that remote forest cave and even, back at the Unawatuna Devale, going on my daily alms round striving to attain the goal".

Those were his thoughts when he was preparing for ordination in Gothama Thapovanaya, but he knew that the majority of monks in Sri Lanka, even at Thapovanaya, where the meditation was mostly for the Westerners, clearly did not share the same immediate ambitions or aspirations and from Eustace in Unawatuna he knew that the native priests had for the most part abandoned the more traditional, austere, meditative Bhikkhu life to engage in scholastic study, social works and even politics. He saw they were obviously not on the same wavelength as he was in his imagination. He had to tolerate the reality surrounding him, and he would. For the time being, it was okay because he had, as a novice monk, to study the *Dhamma* writings anyway, but even during that period, he made use of different places that offered the opportunity for more secluded and ascetic practice.

One of them was a cave located at the base of Dolukhanda mountain in a remote area, about six hours' bus journey from Colombo, with poisonous snakes around and a lot of monkeys. He had to guard against them. It was a challenge on his round trip of one or two miles to collect alms food because the monkeys were forever trying to steal something from his bowl. He knew from a special experience at a temple in Nepal where he had an unexpected and rather frightening encounter with monkeys that inhabited the forested hills around and which the temple was actually named after: the Monkey Temple. Rahula was holding a half-full bag of roasted peanuts when he was ambushed by a gang of large monkeys, to whom he finally had to hand over the nuts.

The cave in Dolukhanda mountain was the location of his most intensive meditation and ascetic practice, where he worked on overcoming fears of various kinds, especially the fear of death.

Another place he visited was Unawatuna. The villagers there were very happy to see him officially in robes now. Meanwhile, he returned to Thapovanaya, reported his progress in meditation to the Venerable Vangisa and stayed two weeks or so studying the Pali Buddhist texts in English translation.

He returned to the United States in 1978 to visit his family and to see how Buddhism was developing in the West. He stayed for most of the time at the International Buddhist Meditation Center on New Hampshire Avenue in Los Angeles, only fifty miles from his parents home in Riverside. The head of the Center was a very respected Vietnamese Zen Master named the Venerable Thich Thien-An, also a professor of Buddhist Philosophy and teaching at Los Angeles City College. Although the center focused predominantly on the *Mahayana* branch of Buddhism, it, as it was mostly comprised of Americans, was keen on having monks and nuns from all the different Buddhist traditions living there together and sharing their traditions with each other. Thien-An was happy to see him. He asked him to stay because the resident *Theravada* monk had just passed away. Rahula began to give *Dhamma* talks on occasion at the Sunday meditation service and teach a yoga and meditation class once a week. Buddhist meditation was starting to become quite popular in America then and increasingly large numbers of people attended these sessions.

It was there, apart from some lessons he once gave on request in Goa, that Bhante Rahula started to give talks on the *Dhamma*. The center was also a place, or as Rahula put it, "a chance" to broaden his understanding of the different *Mahayana* teachings and traditions. A lot of Buddhist ceremonies and festivals were celebrated and teachers from Tibetan, Zen, *Theravada* and other sects dropped by for teaching programs. It was different from his monk's life in Sri Lanka, but at least, for the time being, he enjoyed the change.

On the Vesak day in 1979 he made the final step to fully embracing the monk's life and received his higher ordination (*Upasampada*). The ceremony was held at Wat Thai Buddhist temple in Los Angeles. This temple was founded as the first Thai Buddhist temple in the United States in 1971 and is situated in the Sun Valley, about 15 miles north of downtown Los Angeles. The temple replicates the traditional Buddhist temples in Thailand.

A group of Sri Lankan monks residing in Los Angeles at this time organized the ordination. Rahula's parents and other family members were able to take part in this auspicious event. About six months later, he became, as he said, "kind of homesick" and wanted to go back to his original vision of the "mendicant monk lifestyle in a secluded area" and practice meditation, so, in 1980, he returned to India.

First he went again to Bodh Gaya, meditated under the sacred Bodhi tree and stayed in some of the various monasteries there that offered free hospitality. By making a pilgrimage on foot, he walked to the other holy places connected to the Buddha's life and finished it at Lumbini in Nepal, the birthplace of the Buddha. He went on alms rounds, slept in ashrams, Buddhist temples, or just under trees off the main roads. He continued on to a *Theravada* monastery in Pokhara and made a month-long trek up to the pilgrimage spot of Muktinath and also to the Annapurna Sanctuary. By the middle of January 1981, he was back in Sri Lanka and would stay there for six years.

He spent most of the time in Unawatuna, the spot he had been so fascinated by on his first visit there and had gone on a wonderful, private meditation retreat for a month, at the end of which, his decision to become a monk was no longer in question.

In the three years of his absence, tourists had discovered Unawatuna Bay. Hotels and restaurants along the shoreline and among the village houses disturbed the isolated, tranquil setting he had previously enjoyed on the beach itself. However, there was the Devale at the foot of that little hill and its peak. He discovered the little spot on the peak of the hill that looked so tempting to him for building a Kuti underneath a thick canopy of trees and bushes. The material needed was bought in Galle in the timber yards and other shops selling construction material. Some of the villagers donated all of it and others came up and helped to build. The Kuti had neither water nor electric power, but it did have a kerosene lamp.

When I went up with him, the Kuti was not longer there. It had to be torn down after Rahula left for good because it happened that foreigners had been using it to take drugs and even have sex in. The hill itself had changed immensely. Nowadays there is a large Stupa and an equally large Buddha statue in the middle of the peak plateau, and next to it a Buddhist temple. However, when Rahula had his Kuti there, it was perfect for him. He told me:

"People seldom came up to the top of the hill except to watch the sunset and even then they were usually quiet. The Kuti could not be seen from the outside, so people didn't even know I was there. I had a gap cut in the bushes at the back of the hut which opened out onto the large rocks of the bluff here. As you can see, the waves of the Indian Ocean are just about twenty feet below. And here on a flat rock, I could comfortably sit for meditation, facing the sunset, unseen by others. It was nice and I went on my daily alms round down in different parts of the area."

He became a kind of legend there. Even ages later, when I was walking with him through Unawatuna, there were always people that recognized him, a tuck-tuck driver, say, or a man who was a child back then, and talked to him on the streets. They had seen him for years, a western monk, tall and skinny, on his way through the area, begging for alms, and they knew who he was and where he lived.

Dana, as I have already mentioned, is an old tradition of generosity, an integral part of life in a Buddhist monastery. The term 'Bhikkhu' for monks in Pali means 'someone begging for food'. We know the name in the translation 'mendicant monk'.

When I was with Rahula in Unawatuna, we lived in a guest house that belongs to the family of a woman I knew from my hometown of Hamburg in Germany. She is a member of a Sri Lankan association that was looking for a location for a Buddhist temple and finally founded one in the area of Hamburg. I used to be the chairman of the association and she was always telling me to visit Sri Lanka, where I could live in their guest house. What I knew from her, apart from other things, was that a lot of *Dana* has to be given when it comes to celebrations like Vesak and other holidays with the association members. What I did not know was that, as a twelve-year-old girl, she had cooked a carrot and a potato as a special *Dana* for a tall and skinny western monk every day whenever he was expected to make an appearance on his alms route. She never talked to him at that time because she did not speak English. The monk she saw was, of course, Bhante Rahula, or 'the 'white monk' as they called him in Unawatuna, and he noticed her. In 1995, when he went back for a visit to Unawatuna, he asked the girl's mother about her and heard she was married and lived in Germany. He said that he was often there and that she might be able to contact him. Mali, the girl, now a woman, tried this, but to no avail. Then she met him shortly again in Unawatuna in 2005. At that time, he was there to bring the donation from the USA he had initiated for the repair of the roof of the Devale, which, like every other building in Unawatuna, had been destroyed by the horrible Tsunami in 2004.

One day it so happened that I mentioned to my friend Mali, who I had first met in 2003, that I was going to House of Silence on a meditation retreat with the American monk Bhante Rahula. She was puzzled and since then she gives him *Dana* whenever he is in Hamburg. He also sleeps in her family's house sometimes.

Rahula began to teach regularly in Sri Lanka when he lived in his homemade Kuti in Unawatuna. From there, he once visited a new meditation center in the mountains above Kandy, in

Nilambe. It was mainly founded by a layman named Godwin Samaratne and primarily intended for use by lay people. Anyway, Rahula was asked by Godwin to teach on a ten-day retreat while Godwin, who traveled a lot to teach in different places, was away.

This mountainside center is absolutely secluded without electric power, but with a lot of leeches. Warnings and mindfulness are of no use because you will get leeches from time to time anyway. Not so much in meditation sessions because participants sit on benches with their legs off the ground, but one might inadvertently carry them in and then wonder afterwards why one's feet were so bloody, which is quite a challenge, especially for western participants used to neat and tidy environments during meditation. But meditators like Bhante Rahula, who are used to natural surroundings, have to deal with insects and animals all the time. Leeches are not dangerous and not unhealthy either (just a little disgusting for some), unlike mosquitos or snakes, for example.

Neither are Squirrels dangerous, but it is funny when one of them jumps from a tree onto Rahula's shoulder, as happened in a forest near House of Silence in Roseburg.

Rahula likes to take his students for meditation sessions outside because there are a lot of sensations one can become aware of like, for instance, insects feeding, but the squirrel saw

only something reddish and motionless—
Rahula's robe—on the forest floor and wanted to know what it was.

Rahula was teaching ten-day meditation
courses at Nilambe about two or three times a
year over the five years he mostly spent in
Unawatuna. At that time he did not go back
to Thapovanaya. There was no reason since
his teacher, the Venerable Vangisa, had passed
away.

After the Himalayan hiking tour and the pilgrimage through India, he felt that he wanted
to return to the West and help to spread Buddhism there. That was exactly when he acquired knowledge (not accidently, of course,
because we know there are no accidents) of a
forest monastery and meditation center in the
Theravada tradition that would be opening in
West Virginia.

There was an old owl that sat on an oak
The more he sat the less he spoke
The less he spoke the more he heard
We should be like that wise old bird
Poem about meditation

Chapter 9

In May 1984, a Buddhist monk in America was sitting in a café in West Virginia in the United States. He had an appointment with a real estate agent, who should help him to find a place where the monk could do what he indented to do, to build the first *Theravada* monastery in the United States. For that matter he had collected 18,000 US dollars. But the agent did not show up. The monk's chaperone, an American family father and meditation student, was asking around for the realtor and while doing so, he was asked by one of the customers of the café how many acres would be needed. "About ten to fifteen acres," the friend of the monk who supported the mission answered.

"I have thirteen acres," the man said. "I want 18,000 dollars for it. Are you interested?"

This dialog is from the autobiography of Bhante Gunnaratana, aka Bhante G., who happened to be the monk. This was one of these incidents that we like to call a coincidence; One has exactly the 18,000 dollars that the other is looking for. They made the deal. Bhante G. described it as a beautiful property, thickly covered with trees and a small spring-fed creek trickling through it.

Four years later, the place, although already connected with electricity, was not much more than a wood. Apart from electricity, a well for water had been drilled and the skeleton for a narrow building erected. About that time Bhante G. wrote:

"My only companion in those early days was the Venerable Yogavacara Rahula, a young American monk who had been wandering around Asia and had ordained in the mid-1970 in Sri Lanka. He had heard about our plan to build a forest monastery and wrote to me in Washington, asking if he could join us. He had moved onto the land in April 1987, while I was still in Washington. He lived in the partially completed building. Bhante Rahula would prove, over the years, to be my right-hand man and the most energetic, dependable Bhikkhu I had ever met."

Bhante G.'s intention to erect a forest monastery, meets the intention from Bhante Rahula regarding his life, namely as a "mendicant monk in a secluded area and practicing meditation".

All Bhante G. wanted to see in this new monastery in the secluded isolated mountain valley of West Virginia was „monks, nuns, and lay meditators strolling the path deep in meditation and contemplation of the *Dhamma*". And he hoped that there would be some day as many of them as there were trees in the forest. So it was hardly surprising, after Bhante G. invited Rahula, who was only thinking of staying for one or two weeks, that he stayed for years to come.

In April 1987, he met Bhante G. for the first time in Washington D.C. and from there both of them drove out to the place where only this one shell of a building had then been erected. When Bhante G. and some volunteers were doing some work and spending the night there, they slept in sleeping bags on the floor. When Rahula saw the carcass, he immediately had that kind of feeling: "Yeah, this is the place". Bhante G. took him around and Rahula wanted to do some work and said: "Okay, I'll stay here for, you know, a week or two."

"Yes," Bhante G. told me, when I talked to him about the beginning, "two weeks. He came for two weeks, I remember. And when he came, I asked him to clearing a site for a vegetable garden, for which he had to pick countless rocks out of the mountain soil. When I returned two weeks later, he had used those rocks to build a handsome retaining wall. I thought: This is the kind of hard worker

209

we need to make this place a reality. And I asked why won't you stay here with us?"

Yes, why not? And so the two weeks became 23 years. Rahula quickly felt in love with the area and saw its potential. Thus he began staying on the property full time alone to continue the work, making friends with the sparse neighbors and meditating alone in the forest, which he loves to do so much.

"There was some food," Rahula said, "and there was a little gas cooker there, and a water tap from the well they dug, and electricity, and a toilet was already working. But the building was not finished. There was no insulation inside, there was no carpet on the floor, just the cement floor, but it was quite satisfactory for staying in."

"But there was already a roof?", I asked.

"Yes there was a roof and I stayed there and I made my own breakfast with oranges and oat meal. Bhante G. had introduced me to the neighbors in the back. They arranged some food for me, actually cooked my lunch. I started clearing land because you couldn't walk through the property."

If you come to the Bhavana Society nowadays, you will find a place, even still pretty isolated in the West Virginian area called 'High View', but with a lot of proper buildings with a gem of a meditation hall as a center. Entering the monastery, you pass a little wood shed and to the right, opposite some little offices on the left, you will find the main building, where, connected to it by a corridor at the back, the meditation hall is situated, which was erected as an extension in 1997. Within the wooded area there are now 20 so called Kutis, little huts with one room and heating, but without water and electricity, apart from two, plus four houses for residents. Altogether there is currently accommodation for about 60 people.

The monastery seems to me like a 'work in progress'. When I was there for the first time in 2008, I stayed in the then first Kuti with electricity, the Apanada. That was very well located for me, just behind the guest house, where I needed to go to use the bathroom. When I returned in 2015, this guest house had been replaced by a roomier one with a suitable modern interior. Anyway, every building to be erected or maintained and every development of the estate, let alone its expansion, depends on the *Dana*. Hence the money and help from the people. In 1987, Matthew Flickstein, a loyal friend and moreover the companion who was with Bhante G. when they got the offer for the place, bought an additional ten acres near the monastery and another supporter a two-acre strip that lay between the two tracts. Both places were donated to the monastery that owned then a total of twenty-five acres. Nowadays it covers about forty-two.

The first building was finished in different stages in accord with the money that was available. It had been completed, with a small meditation room along with all the basic infrastructure, by the fall of 1988. Also an office building across from the main house was erected then. Before the opening ceremony of the *Bhavana Society Forest Monastery and Meditation Center* in October, a first retreat had already taken place, called a 'tent retreat' according to Bhante Rahula, since the 15 to 20 participants were sleeping in tents they had brought with them.

About the ceremony Bhante Rahula said: "A lot of people came, more than 300, including 24 monks and 4 nuns and members from Bhavana Society, and also the sheriff."

"The sheriff?"

"Yes the Sheriff of Hampshire County. He was the special guest. We invited him to cut the ribbon. He was wearing his uniform and gun because he was on duty. But he was very nice."

"Did he give a speech as well?"

"He gave a little talk. Like welcoming us and so on."

Apart from the main building, three wooden Kutis off in the forest had been erected as well. Every single Kuti is named and one of it has the name *Rahula*. He built it by himself and later used to live in it. Of course, it was a much more stable version than the one he had before in Unawatuna. However, you can say he kind of became used to it. Anyway, it was necessary to have dwelling places and so it was on his mind from the beginning, when he was walking through the area, to build some Kutis off from the main building and looking for proper spots. And one them he found he wanted to have for himself.

"So," he said. "I got the ideas and I started clearing the areas and making a trail, outlining through the forest a kind of loop to the spots where the Kutis should be. Then Bhante G. found a guy who volunteered to donate money for a Kuti. First I started with my Kuti. It happened there was some guy, a local fellow, who came by and introduced himself. He was actually a carpenter. I asked him some questions and talked about the ideas I had. So I gradually built that Kuti; I think, it took me about a month and then another guy came and also built one for Bhante G., or better, he hired somebody to do that. And this other guy, who helped Bhante G. with the land, this Matthew Flickstein, also had a Kuti built for himself. There were others helping to finish the main building and they erected the office house."

It took a lot of work to develop the monastery and Bhante Rahula was from the beginning the one that had contributed plenty of it. When, in 1997, the new meditation hall was erected, Bhante G. was calling Rahula "our architect". He had asked him four years earlier to plan a meditation hall and the plan Bhante Rahula drew up was later approved by the professional architect.

The hall is wonderful. A cathedral-like pine structure with a floor heating system for the really cold West Virginia winters. At the front stands a massive Buddha statue on a high altar in front of a stained-glass window that shows an image of a Bhodi tree leaf. Coming at five o'clock in the morning into the hall, it gives you, in the inspiring candle twilight, a spiritual atmosphere for common early morning meditation.

In the beginning, Rahula said, the people around, the neighbors, where a little skeptical about what to make of the place because Buddhism was not very well known in the mid-eighties. They had some bad publicity from other cults, and other religions, but over the years most people have come to accept it.

Being responsible for a functional monastery seems similar to running a company. There is an office for the administration staff to manage the assignments, to care for nutrition and handle maintenance, even a holiday per week for the inhabitants. About the latter, Bhante Rahula smiled when we talked about it and said that that happened much later, when there were more monks and training. I mentioned it because I saw a day-off schedule on the bill board as well as a duty plan. The Bhavana Society is not only a place were monks live but is also open as a residence for lay people. People come for different reasons, often to see if it may prove suitable for them to become a monk or nun themselves or just to live in the secluded environment of a monastery and help with daily chores. It also happens that now and then residents come just to hide. In the beginning when every hand was needed, Kathy Nally, the secretary, checked the driver license of one of them and realized there was a warrant from the state of Florida because he had not paid some parking tickets. Or another guy, who, as it turned out later, came to escape from his wife to avoid paying child support. It also occurred once that a resident, who had been given the monastery credit card to buy groceries, not only stole it and used it later in different states but also actually stole a car that belonged to a mother of one of the monks. But those were rare exceptions; most of the lay people were alright and the monastery in a way needs them, especially for cooking or going shopping. However, unusual things are not only limited to the laity. Once, it occurred that a nun started to meet a male resident in the woods, which is forbidden in the precepts for both nuns and monks. So she had to leave and, over the years, the monastery has had to let at least three nuns and two monks go. Not only for the same reason, but also for being angry or arguing with decisions taken. As I have said, running a monastery is not merely limited to religious affairs or developing the *Dhamma*, but must also take care of the usual worries that are common to living and working in any society.

In *Theravada*, there is not really a hierarchy as there is in *Mahayana* like, for example, in Tibet about which the whole world knows the Dalai Lama is ostensibly the highest priest, which, as a matter of fact, is incorrect. He is actually only one out of four of the religious highest leaders of different spiritual schools in Tibet. His appearance of superiority derives from his being represented, as the leader of that sect, as the secular leader of the nation of Tibet. In *Theravada*, the life of a monk is reckoned according to how many *Vassa* he has spent. *Vassa* means rain and refers to the monsoon season between July and October. The monks are not supposed to be on walks or travels during that period; they must stay in a fixed place such as a monastery. If a monk is ordained in June, he can say he has 'one rain' even though a period of twelve months has not yet passed. However, if a monk is ordained in November of that same year, he has to wait until the next year before he can say that he has one rain. This is the rule in terms of seniority in a monastery or a center; for example, where they stand in a line or sit when eating. The oldest monk or nun is always the one at the front, sitting at the front. In the Bhavana Society, Bhante G. was the oldest and also the abbot. Bhante Rahula was the vice abbot. However, as much he liked to work in the monastery, especially when creating something in the area, he was not really happy with the responsibility that came with living in a monastery.

For most people it came as a surprise when, in 2010, he left Bhavana and they wanted to know why. It was simply that he wanted to be free of a monk's life with all its responsibilities, especially when thinking about the future: in his case, maybe becoming the abbot one day. The year before he left, Bhante G. took a sabbatical and for that year Bhante Rahula could experience, at first hand, the meaning of being fully in charge. In a society, even a monastery, it is inevitable that tensions appear. You have to deal with them and, as a monk, you have to do so in the mindful way appropriate to the character of a monk.

There were some tensions between some of the board members during Bhante G.s sabbatical., hence some wrongs were committed and some bad decisions made. They showed Bhante Rahula that to be in charge was not his main intention. The proof of it came when the board allowed an unsuitable layman to stay on. That man caused some problems and Bhante Rahula was blamed for allowing him to stay.

Why Bhante Rahula left Bhavana after twenty-three years in which he, at least as far as I know, had a gratifying time, in which such incidents as the above-mentioned were unimportant, is perhaps best explained by a friend from Germany, the physician Klaus Habich, who, with his wife Miyako, attended almost every Christmas retreat of the Bhavana-Society from 1994 to 2009:

"In the Bhavana Society, Rahula was very different. Here in Germany, he seemed to me more relaxed. There, he was stricter, because the responsibility was a burden to him. The relationship between him and Bhante G. as well as with the other monks naturally remained concealed from me. However, over the years it was noticeable that there must have been considerable tensions there, at least at times. I think Bhante Rahula was kind of oppressed in the Bhavana society – he could not do as he wanted."

And yes, there is a kind of bureaucracy around life in the monastery—I have experienced it myself—and it may be necessary. However, for someone mostly interested in developing the *Dhamma* with meditation and studies, it is not always appropriate. However, in answer to the question why he left, he gave me the same one Bhavana's secretary, Kathy, gave me when I asked her about it:

"He now has what he wanted to do his whole life: to be a wandering monk and go around spreading the *Dhamma*. His decision was caused by his never wanting to shoulder so much responsibility. To be an abbot or vice-abbot is like leading a company or something, with a lot of things that have to be managed and I think it wasn't what he really wanted to do." And she added: "When he returned after his one year release from Bhavana, I could see he was more relaxed and brighter and his decision to go away was the right thing for him".

With the hard work and ascetic life in the secluded area where the monastery is located, Rahula, for a certain time, could combine the two aspects he wanted to have in his life: the first was to be a mendicant monk, dwelling in a remote forest. For people like me, this is not only connected with discomfort, but also with how to deal the wild-life and I wanted to know from him how the situation in the hills of West Virginia was in this regard.

"Yeah," he said, "the most dangerous animals were rattlesnakes. Apart from them, there were just deer and they aren't dangerous. Or other small animals like opossum and so on. That was really nice, living in a place close to so many deer. But it also reminds me that sometimes hunters came to hunt in this area. And one day, it was a Thanksgiving day, November 25, there was about a foot of snow on the ground and me and Bhante G., myself and the monk named Sona, who was the first, by the way, to be ordained here, were standing after breakfast together talking, when we suddenly heard *Bum-Bum*. Shots, you know. It was kind of loud and a minute later we saw a deer running down; it was trailing blood and the blood left red marks on the fresh white snow. Very clearly. And then, a few minutes later two hunters came, carrying guns, following the track of blood. We asked: "what are you doing?" And they said: "we shot that deer" and we told them that they were on our property and that the rules were that if they shot a deer and it ran onto a property, you had to let it go. But they demanded to follow insisted on pursuit because it was wounded and they had to finish it off because otherwise it would suffer. So what could we do? We didn't want to get them angry. They had guns and all. And they were determined and argued they would have the right to kill it anyway. Later we put up 'No Trespassing' signs all over the place."

The second aspect for Bhante Rahula, what he wanted in his life, was to spread Buddhism in the West. In order to achieve that, he did not limit his ministry to the monastery in West Virginia but traveled around, mostly to Europe, but also to Asia and South America to teach. It was in the same year, when Bhavana opened, actually the summer before, that Rahula first travelled for teaching purposes to Europe. He had at that time invitations from Buddhist centers in the northern part of

Germany that were extended to him in 1986 when he crossed Europe on his way back from Sri Lanka to the United States. First he went to Berlin, where he had already been in 1977 on his first return from Asia to the USA when he was still a novice. He traveled through Europe and, in Croatia, he met Asha and Keshav Rekai, who happened to run a Yoga school in West-Berlin. They invited him there and drove him to Berlin. They became two of his closest friends but passed away recently. In Berlin he came into contact with the *Buddhist House* in Frohnau, a suburb of Berlin. From there he went to Hesberj Peace Center near Odense, Denmark at the invitation of a man named Mr. Vig. This man, who runs the center, once went to Sri Lanka to meet Bhante Rahula's teacher Vangisa at the Gothama Thapovanaya monastery. He wanted to start a Buddhist center on his land, which he called a World Peace Centre. Bhante Vangisa then went to Denmark, brought a Buddhist statue and taught there. He actually wanted Bhante Rahula to do this, who, however, did not feel ready at that time. Anyway, in 1986 he spent the summer there. He tried to conduct a couple of courses, but the place was more a venue for hippies, who were taking drugs and playing music, and only a few people came. It did not really work out in terms of trying to establish a Buddhist center there.

However, two visitors happened to have a big influence in his further teaching travels. It was a couple from Hamburg in Germany, Karin and Holger Börnsen. I met them later (2003), when I came into contact with the BGH, the Buddhistische Gesellschaft Hamburg (Buddhist Society of Hamburg), for which I then went on to publish the printed quarterly Buddhist magazine for years. In 1986, Karin Börnsen was actually the chairwoman of the BGH. She told me about the trip to Denmark that she and her husband took on bicycles and it must have been a kind of adventure because they did not find the venue straightaway and had to sleep in hay in a nearby farm and use a cow trough for their morning toilet. When the next day they finally found the isolated old farm with almost nothing but hippies on it, the monk they had come to see was not there. This was the second time they had tried to meet him since Karin and Holger had just missed him on an earlier trip to Unawatuna. There on that little hill overlooking the Devale, they stumbled across his Kuti, hopping to meet him while they were there, but he was not around. Back in Hamburg, they heard he was in Denmark and decided to take another chance, but again to no avail. Anyway, this time they left an invitation letter and one day, after short notice, he showed up and, when I visited her and Holger one day, Karin said about the first meeting with Bhante Rahula:

"He immediately sat himself on the bench, where you are sitting now, in the lotus posture. Easily, like a bird. I really got a heart-throb when he arrived, but he was sitting there and smiling, did not say so much and neither did I. I got a little tense about the silence until I thought, what is it that you actually want? And then I became very calm in his presence. He had wonderful energy."

She invited some Buddhist friends right away for the evening and Bhante Rahula was performing a 'seminar', as he called it, in the living room. Later Karin brought him to the BGH for meditation practice and lectures This center was, at the suggestion of the Singhalese monk Narada Mahathera and some Buddhists from Hamburg, founded in 1954 and has been located at its present site since 1980. It was created, as the statute says, as an association of persons recognizing the teachings of the historic Buddha, as laid down in the Pali Canon. The center is open to all schools of Buddhism. In the house there are two rooms for meditation or other events, a proper library and, on the second floor, rooms of residence for monks, nuns and other teachers. Narada Mahathera took over the patronage first, followed by Ayya Khema in 1987 and in 1998 by Bhante Seelawansa, who lives in Vienna.

By the members of the BGH, Bhante Rahula was also invited to the *House of Silence* in

Roseburg, the place where I first met him. This venue is one of the oldest Buddhist meditation centers in Germany. Located approximately 50 km east of Hamburg, in the direction of Berlin. It is surrounded by an area rich in ponds and quiet forests. The place has a main house erected in the 'twenties of the last century, a modern guest house and a meditation hall next to a little pond and creek in the midst of greenery and trees. The house has been used as a meditation center since 1962. Seminars are suitable for first-time participants as well as for those who have been practicing for many years. The *House of Silence* is also open to all schools of Buddhism, and it is not necessary to identify with Buddhist ideas or principles in order to participate. The place offers accommodation for up to 38 seminar participants in simply furnished single and multi-bed rooms. The available food resources are vegetarian. The House of Silence is running by a non-profit association and financed by membership fees, donations and seminar contributions.

There Rahula met Frank, who, as he told me, was immediately impressed by him and enthusiastic about his stupendous teaching ability, asked him right away to teach a course and they made a plan for 1988. That is why he went to Hamburg already in the summer of 1988, even the Bhavana Society had not been opened by then. In that year, first he gave a session for a week in the BGH in Hamburg, before conducting the *Vipassana* meditation retreat in the House of Silence and, after that, went to Berlin to visit the *Buddha House* and gave some lectures there, which he continued to do so in the years to come as well as in the Yoga school of his friends.

The *Buddhist House* was founded in 1924. Thus it is the oldest Buddhist center in Europe. Its existence was curtailed when the Nazis came to power in Germany in 1933. After the Second World War, it first gave shelter to refugees and then fell into ruin due to the lack of money for its physical maintenance, let alone its continuance as a Buddhist temple. Even demolition was considered. In 1957, however, Asoka Weeraratna, a businessman from Sri Lanka, learned about it. He was affected by Germany losing so many citizens during the war, being confronted with the problem of departed families and vanished property. It seemed to him that there might be a thirst for a moral-spiritual alternative emphasizing peace and non-violence, compassion and *Metta*. He founded the *German Dhammaduta Society,* in whose name he bought the house in December 1957. Since then, the *Dhamma* has been taught at events and meditation seminars again.

The site is reminiscent of temples in Sri Lanka: situated on a hill with a steep staircase of seventy-four steps. At the foot above the gate is the inscription *The Buddhist House.* It is located right next where the Berlin wall was erected. When I was later on a walk with Bhante Rahula in this area with its neat environment, he was reminded of that earlier time, walking on a dirt road at the back of the temple while all the time meeting army jeeps on patrol.

In Berlin, the 275-kilometer-distant city of Hamburg and the village of Roseburg, situated between the two biggest cities in Germany, everybody asked him to come back and so he did, every year. Meanwhile, he met Paul Köppler, who runs Forest House (*Waldhaus*) at the Laacher See, a meditation center near Bonn, founded in 1986. Bhante Rahula added that to his list of venues to visit in Germany and, little by little, he was also invited by others. The locations in Allgäu in the southern part of Germany near the Alps are also worth mentioning.

The *Buddha House,* about 15 kilometers from Kempten in Allgäu, is a seminar house, but also an extensive spiritual project. It was founded in 1989 on the initiative of the German Buddhist nun and meditation teacher, the recognized Ayya Khema. The task of the project is to spread the teachings of the Buddha. The spiritual director is Bhante Nyanabodhi. Located nearby, also among meadows and forests, is the *Metta Vihara Forest Monastery* (Waldkloster), which belongs to the Buddha

House. It was also started by Ayya Khema, just before she passed away in 1997. The present abbot is Bhante Nyanabodhi, who happens to be a direct disciple of hers. It is a monastery in the *Theravada* tradition. Only a few kilometers from the *Buddha House* is the *Anenja Vihara*. It is a monastery for Buddhist nuns and lay women. The current Abbess, since 2010, is Ayya Sucinta, who was, by the way, ordained as a novice nun by Bhante G. at the Bhavana Society in the late 'nineties. She took Bhikkhuni ordination in Bodh Gaya, India.

Also in the tradition of the teaching of Ayya Khema is the *Lotus Vihara Meditation Centre* (Lotos-Vihara Meditationszentrum) that is not situated in Allgäu but in Berlin. It is surrounded by a beautiful garden and, in the center of the big city, a meditative oasis for quiet and contemplation and open to the public. So Bhante Rahula also added it to the venues he would visit when coming to Germany. There were still other places in Germany, too. However, Bhante Rahula's teaching trips are not limited to Germany since he had already gone from Berlin to Paris for some consecutive annual events in 1989. The time he spent in Europe extended from one month to two months, even three months, with stays in Austria, Switzerland and Sweden, to name but a few of the countries. For about ten years he came back every year and then Bhante G., who went for teaching purposes every year to Brazil, asked Bhante Rahula to go as well and split the years between them to be in Brazil. Therefor he reduced his trips to Europe to a two-years rhythm. He has held to that rhythm even after leaving the Bhavana Society. Nevertheless he has added other countries like the Czech Republic or Romania to his itinerary, for example.

But he not only visited Europe and Brazil but also Asia, especially Sri Lanka and India. No longer burdened by monastic responsibilities, he expanded his travels especially to Asia for months and sometimes spent the *Vassa* there. He visits Buddhist monasteries and centers and teaches from time to time. And, of course, he still does his beloved trekking tours.

Thankfully Bhante Rahula has installed an Internet website/blog where he put his whereabouts, travels, retreat schedules, photos, videos and audio files. It makes it very helpful for his students all over the world to follow his steps and know where he will be and hold a retreat or seminar and attend conferences etc. Especially for his friends and students from Europe since he decided after 2017 to break with coming here every second year. He might come back sometimes, but one cannot tell when. There are manifold reasons for that sad decision that affect every center in Europe as well as his students, who love to have him as a teacher. One is he just wants to be in America because of his aging mother and, not least, it has to do with his own age probably as well. His mother turned 99 in that year and he 70.

Another aspect is his new position as director and principal meditation teacher at the new 'Lion of Wisdom' Meditation Center, located between Baltimore, Maryland and Washington, DC. It has been established in memory of Ven. Madihe Pannsiha Mahanayaka Thera, the founder of the Washington Buddhist Vihara, which in 1965 was the first *Theravada* Buddhist temple in the USA.

The 'Lion of Wisdom' Meditation Center is a brain-child of Bhante M. *Dhamma*siri, who has been at the Vihara for thirty years. First functioning as secretary and after a year succeeding Bhante G. as president, who then went in 1988 as abbot to the Bhavana Society. The name *Lion of Wisdom* was, according to the center's website, picked as the translation of the Pali word Pannasiha. Panna means wisdom and Siha is a lion. The Lion is the fearless king of animals, while Wisdom is the fearless king of the mind. The combined Vesak and opening ceremony of the new center was held on May 21st, 2017.

However, the house needed repair and renovations before it was suitable for holding short retreats and accommodating overnight guests. In April 2018, Bhante Rahula started conducting *A Day of Mindfulness*, followed in May with a short weekend retreat.

Being a monk means dealing with a lot of matters that differ from ordinary life or, in other words, there is a lack of affairs that people normally have to face. A *Theravada* Bhikkhu is officially allowed only eight requisite items for his private daily use. These are: three robes (two outer and one under-robe), an alms bowl, a needle and thread, a water strainer, a razor, and a belt (to hold up the under-robe). The extra outer robe and other things can be easily packed inside the alms bowl which has a carried bag: in this way, the mendicant Bhikkhu can wander about with all his worldly possessions in one convenient compact bundle. I asked Bhante Rahula what the toughest thing was for him on becoming a monk.

"I don't know", he said, "it is not really tough, but things were very dramatic like shifting from drugs and just running around being a hippie to following the *Dhamma*. It wasn't really that tough but it was the most dramatic shift in my lifestyle."

"So," I persisted, "you didn't have problems with anything else on changing over to life as a monk?"

"No," he said, "there weren't any. I was in Sri Lanka then. Trying to become a monk in America might have been more difficult than in Sri Lanka because you are automatically cut off from all of this. – I mean the environment is totally different."

"And when you came back to the United States, was there anything then?"

"Well, there was maybe some little bit of lure and temptation, but it was not really strong enough."

A monk is not supposed to have money. As a resident of a monastery or a temple, however, a monk's every need is taken care of by the institution in question. If not, a monk or nun is authorized to have a person that would accept donations bona fide for him or her for buying what is needed. Even on journeys, normally monks and nuns take food and so on with them in order not to need to buy anything.

"But once in a while," Rahula said, "nowadays you get stuck in the airport and delayed, and other things like that happen so that you have to take an additional train or bus. So sometimes I do have a little bit of cash for use in case of emergency. Not very often. But you have to avoid giving into the desire to buy chocolate or something. Some monks follow the rule very strictly and others are somewhere in between, and some don't follow it at all. Where I usually stay, the center or friends take care of this."

Although he travels a lot, it is only possible

with an invitation from centers or monasteries. It is the same with friends. They must invite him. And they do. While he is travelling around from center to center, he takes the occasion to visit friends. He said to me:

"When I am with friends, they ask what I would like to see and suggest maybe we should go here or there and then they organize the trip and then we go. Like you did with our trip to Neu-Schwanstein."

Yes, we were in that famous fairytale castle built by King Ludwig II. Over all the years traveling around, Bhante Rahula has met a large number of students. A lot of them take every occasion to see him again and again. The times I was with him in the *House of Silence* (from 1999 to 2017), I guess half of the classes were regulars. Some of them, and from other retreats as well, followed him to retreats that he gave at other places and some became friends and traveled together with him not only for meditation purposes, although at least as far as I am concerned, meditation is always part of it when traveling with him. I guess that is the same with other friends and journeys. On one of the journeys I took the chance to go with him in 2015, it was on the occasion when he went to Allgäu for the ordination of a nun in the Metta Vihara Forest Monastery. Bhante G. was also there and ordained a German nun and it happened to be the first ordination of a nun in the *Theravada* tradition in Europe.

On that occasion, we traveled around and I was lucky to drive both Bhante G. and Bhante Rahula around; apart from other visits to Schloss Neuschwanstein that, for me was the first time. However, Bhante Rahula had been there before. We also visited the Catholic monastery Ottobeuren and met a monk who talked to us about life there and was very pleased to have such visitors as the both Buddhist monks. It was not the first time that we had gone to a Christian monastery. When we were in Waldhaus at Laacher See in 2005, we took the chance to visit the monastery Maria Laach, where we were also greeted by a monk who gave us information and showed a film about the monastery.

Not having money is for a monk, of course, a way to avoid greed, but it also means not being able to support oneself and relying on donations from others. Traditionally in Buddhist countries, lay people believe they improve their *Karma* by giving to monasteries and monks or nuns. This notion of *Dana* is indeed also practiced in the West.

Another aspect that distinguishes a monk's life from that of lay people is not getting close to women or touching them, like holding hands or something like that. I asked Bhante Rahula how problematic this was for him and he said:

"I was never obsessed by this too much. Of course I had girlfriends. But, the idea of getting

233

married was never on my mind. when I was twelve years old, I even told my father that I would never get married. But, yes, there was some desire. You might miss a little pleasure from the experience, but all the planning and mental scheming and how you're gonna meet this girl and when could be the best time, and all this stuff that goes on in your mind, in my mind and in most people's minds it's something I've really never got into. I was not so crazy about another person to get myself attached to them, you know. I really mean the pressure you might get from the contact."

"Yes, I see, but there is another aspect there, the physical. How was it when you felt the need of the body to be with a woman or to have sexual intercourse?"

"I used some of the techniques that the Buddha taught, like the way of pros and cons. Or practicing meditation or yoga…"

"Are there exercises, special exercises?"

"Yeah, you could say they reduce a kind of desire. They called it *Brahma Sharia Mudra*, but it is a complicated exercise."

"Ah. But mostly the way of pros and cons, which also work for other attachments, as you said, right?"

"Yes, naturally in the beginning there is a kind of attraction and thoughts about what might come. But also how much suffering can be involved in a relationship. For some physical pleasure, like having sex, you might find all the other problems. I always tried to think about that and tried to see what a freeing experience it is to be a monk."

"Would you call it then 'Right Intention' that one step of the Noble Eightfold Path?"

"No, it's more like 'Right Thought'. Investigation of the *Dhamma*. To see the reality behind and how to lose desires and so on. When I was in Sri Lanka, in Unawatuna, when it first started to become a tourist place, I saw the European girls taking off their tops when I came down from my Kuti across the beach to collect alms. I tried to visualize these women there as skeletons or deformed in some way in order to see it that way rather than allowing my mind to get caught up in the surface details. It helped a lot."

So that, not having contact to the opposite sex and not having money, are very helpful for the process of mindfulness. From an on-looker's point of view, it could also be considered boring. No fun. However, Rahula had chosen to become happy in serenity and in this way is walking the Noble Eightfold Path.

"Do you ever think you'll stop being a monk?", I asked him once.

"Who knows? I don't say 'never' to anything."

How could I expect another answer? However, I wanted to know if someone decides to do so, what has a monk or nun to do then?

"It is easy, you're only supposed to go to your teacher, but if your teacher is no longer alive or otherwise unavailable, you can go to any other monk, take your robe and say: I relinquish the monk's life and ask for the five precepts. That is all. It is not a big thing. But some people don't do that. But that is not considered right. And then you can't ordain again. That is the rule. If you hadn't asked for the precepts and wanted to become a monk again later, that would be a kind of a problem."

"That sounds easy," I said.

"Yeah, not actually difficult to do it but the decision to do it, you know, probably is."

Living the life of a monk needs mindfulness as it is one of the king pins in life anyway. Every one of Bhante Rahula's students knows this. In his teaching, it runs like a golden thread through all sessions and lectures. Mindfulness is the beginning of the awareness of what happens at a certain moment. Be here now. This term is becoming a very popular kind of slogan. Back in the '60s, the American spiritual teacher and author, Ram Dass, published his famous book *Be Here Now* and it is most likely that, when people heard this phrase for the first time, it started to be used worldwide.

"So we're talking about that", said Bhante Rahula in his retreats, "and, you know it's easy to say 'be here now', be in the present moment, but actually how do we do that?"

The answer a lot of people have found is *Vipassana.* It started as such roughly at the same time as the burgeoning *Vipassana* or Mindful Movement, which was not in the least influenced by Goenka, who was enjoying increasing popularity. Other popular teachers are Jack Kornfield, Susan Salzberg, Jon Kabat-Zinn and Joseph Goldstein. The last of these, by the way, had a great influence on me with his book *Vipassana,* which gave me the idea to go on a retreat in the *House of Silence* at the outset.

According to Rahula, the representatives of the movement water down the *Dhamma.* Their practice of meditation is primarily mindfulness tending towards the psychological rather than the spiritual aspect. One of the main focuses is to use mindfulness to transform the negative tendencies of the mind and to minimize and help deal with pain, stress, worry, anxiety and fear. However, from the deeper *Dhamma* view the experience is of letting go of the ego consciousness to see the true non-dual pure nature of the mind/consciousness.

Although he also gives talks on the aspect mentioned above—Bhante Rahula teaches the *Dhamma* and mindfulness, using *Vipassana* meditation in the sense of the *Satipatthana Sutta.* After that, the four foundations of mindfulness are the primary teachings on meditation leading to the development of insight wisdom, namely seeing reality as it is. The techniques of *Vipassana* meditation are based on these teachings. The four foundations are: mindfulness of the body, the feeling, the mind and the concentration of the *Dhamma.*

In the teachings of the *Satipatthana Sutta,* there is a gradual and systematic approach to training consciousness to stay more grounded and connected in the present moment by using the body as a foundation because it is the only thing that is always with us in the present moment. Bhante Rahula once put it like this: mindfulness of the body serves as a training, as you might train a dog. He said: "Let's say you have a wild and untamed dog that runs out barking and chasing down the street after cyclists or cars and rummaging in trashcans, chasing the other dogs around … So in the same way our mind is like that untrained dog, chasing people around and barking at them … It means chasing our memory of the past and generating thoughts of ill-will towards this or that person or chasing a future that is not here. Or poking your nose into other people's business that doesn't belong to you, or caring what other people are saying about you. All of this is unnecessary, because we allow our minds to stray and get caught up in things that are not important to us at a deep level."

It is the mind that is wandering between the

past and the future and losing its connection to the present moment. The mind, as Bhante Rahula put it in an interview he gave recently on Romanian television that can be followed on YouTube, is probably the most mysterious phenomenon in the universe. Buddhist psychology distinguishes between consciousness and the activities of consciousness. The mind refers to both. Consciousness may be the light that allows us to be aware of both, but the actual mental content consists of feeling, perception, recognition, memories and delusion. Those are the objects of consciousness itself.

At the highest level of meditation, consciousness can be aware without the content of individual objects. Then the consciousness is in pure awareness without any objects, even without a sense of the self. In that interview, he was confronted with theories by psychologists, like Freud, who maintain that being in pure awareness without any objects is only possible when the body dies. They claim that the body gives us stimuli and perceptions every second of our lives and the mind cannot escape from this; in other words, modern psychology ignores that possibility.

"That's the meaning of ignorance," said Bhante Rahula, "it ignores the facts or ignores the truth in this sense because modern scientists or psychologists do not practice meditation at any deeper level. They have not cultivated the faculties to discern the subtlest vibration of consciousness without objects. It cannot be measured with scientific instruments or gadgets."

The main reason, when it comes down to answering the question what is gained by becoming a monk, is that there is a constant ability to be mindful instead of living in the humdrum of a lay life. Others have only the chance in retreats and seminars and that is the reason students of Bhante Rahula become regulars and even follow him around the world. They have probably heard many of his instructions or teachings at least a couple of times. But that is not the point. It is to practice and to continue to practice.

It is of course possible, and every student is encouraged to practice in daily life at home as well, but, as Bhante Rahula also said in that interview, meditating in a group setting, especially for Western students, affords more discipline to achieve this. The technique is not difficult, whereas the discipline required to do it is, namely sitting still for a long time (and maybe experiencing painful stimuli as well) or getting bored or restless. Knowing this as a teacher, he gives the participants of his seminars a helpful practice: the M&M. It stand for 'minute meditation' and means pausing for a minute of mindfulness.

You train yourself to pause, freeze and stop for one minute once an hour. Whether you are sitting or standing, whatever you are doing, just stop the physical activity and feel your feet pressing the floor, take a slow deep breath and relax. Let go of what's going on in the mind and come back to the physical reality of the present moment or Now. You can simply remind yourself of, 'standing breathing, standing breathing, standing breathing'. Or at the same time, you could also forgive anybody who had hurt you in the last hour and send out Metta. You remain like this for one minute and then mindfully continue what you were doing. You try to do this at least once an hour throughout the day. This will help reduce stress hour by hour instead of allowing it to accumulate as most people do. This practice will get you at least ten minutes of valuable meditation or 'mental rest'. This practice will be of a great benefit especially if you cannot manage to get in longer meditations in the morning or evening. This will prove to be a tremendous help.

Without meditation there is no pure awareness. The mind of the average person is constantly active. The initial step in meditation is learning how to wear down the activity of the mind and be more centered in the present moment. Attending a retreat for practice over a longer period of time, undisturbed by outside activities, affords a greater ability to develop a deeper level of mindful tranquility. It usually takes time and many years of practice to gradually become able to control the activities of the mind and develop those deeper levels of awareness. Referring to this, Bhante Rahula said:

"The goal of meditation should not be to

immediately access those deeper states. Rather it is recommended to understand how the mind gets trapped in patterns of thinking, speaking and reacting; to purify one's karmic actions so that you can reach a state of being mindfully at peace with oneself and others. Calming the ego-driven mind comes first. Then you'll be more ready to go on to experience deeper levels of liberation."

Epilog

The Forest Master

In my early days, a book that I appreciated very much was Henry D. Thoreau's *Walden - My Life in the Woods*. This *is* a very fascinating book, which still has an influence on me. Since that time, I've called myself a nature boy or an outdoor person! Buddhist stories are often stories from countryside, groves and forests. I would like to introduce here an American Gentleman, a Buddhist monk who lives in the forest. His course of life is not so much influenced by things like the status of school, study – or profession, but more by his own agenda. His life is determined by the art of mindfulness: where morality is not a question of interpretation, but a very clear thing, like piercing the dark from with light. He is inspired to understand life itself and according to that, the life of everybody else. A part of this is to understand one's own life as a part of nature, to be connected in every breath with the whole.

It is no exaggeration to say that this monk is the archetype of a master, a wise man, who lives alone and far from the crowd, but accepts invitations and comes to lead us to truth and inner growth.

His life as a monk demonstrates the clarity and the shine of Dharma. Appearances like Bhante Rahula are rare. You truly imagine him as the successor and son of Buddha. He is authentic. You can see it in the posture of his body. He does everything slowly; you see it in small gestures, this minimal motion, not doing too much, only as much as necessary, where the patience of the hurried, normal person would be challenged. Whenever I see Rahula, I think of the old wise Hindus. Their respect for all creatures, for animals and plants. You could talk of an attitude of humility and modesty—an attitude characteristic of wise human beings and perhaps the most permanent form of happiness.

Educated in the severe discipline of Vinaya, this monk is a homeless person who has achieved mental freedom and who can demonstrate with his whole person—also with his body—the truth. Radula's mother country is America. The story starts in California in the 'forties, where Scott DuPrez—Bhante Rahula's bourgeois name—spent his childhood. But his home is the Dharma. That is where he is at home. After his education as a Yogi and Theravada monk, after long years of pilgrimage and wandering in India and Sri Lanka, where he lived in caves and woods, wandering in pathless regions alone and on foot in the Himalayas, he returned to America. To make life simple and to understand his essence, Rahula lives in the remote wilderness of the Shenandoah Valley, in the *mirth* of stone mountains, woods and rushing streams. It is part of his nature that his hut (built by himself) where he splits wood and carries water and where the light comes from an oil-lamp, is furthest away from the Bhavana monastery.

Bhante Rahula lives a life of simplicity and renunciation in the tradition of the old school of Buddhism and it is one of his most prominent characteristics that he gets his strength and his *terseness* just from this self-limitation, from this renunciation. At the same time, it is very peculiar that such a lonesome wanderer has more community spirit than those speaking about such things. So he is admired by his pupils not only as a monk and a meditation master, but also for his human personality. He is born to be a friend and because of his unconditional *heartiness* his friendships tends to be ever-enduring.

What can we learn from Rahula? He personifies the true Dharma with all his human strength. To meet him is like entering an old forest, where we are allowed to breathe deeply and become healthy. The main spirit in that is the art of the successful life, where no confusing thoughts torment and where the heart is without doubt. This understanding is the foundation of his life and it is always his *aim* to make the wonderful Dharma clear. We can learn from him in a very detailed manner how to achieve calm and relinquish all over stimulating activities; not how to exist, but to experience existence itself, which is audible in this silence. This generates a natural resonance in us. It is like a spiritual rebirth, where *emotion and reason* are in harmony. In this is strength and courage; there is nothing to fear and we can be more composed, simple and happy—a source of warmth and strength for others. This experience should reflect on the world, should become relevant individually and in society, because the *wear and tear of human beings* and the environment cannot be a matter of indifference to us.

Mahathera Yogavacara Rahula cannot be reduced to vice-abbot, Yoga and meditation teacher. He has many talents and is a learned man who can work as a manual worker, too. The meditation hall, made entirely of wood, was built by him, and you can also see here the clarity of the essence that he himself radiates. His example of how to live, which connects freshness and directness with the mature pragmatism of a wise man, is the perfect practice of them, which we highly recommend.

Frank Wesendahl
December 2009